ALSO BY KIM SAVAGE

Beautiful Broken Girls

After the Woods

IN HER SKIN

IN HER SKIN

Kim Savage

SQUARE
FISH

FARRAR STRAUS GIROUX · NEW YORK

SQUARE
FISH

An imprint of Macmillan Publishing Group, LLC
175 Fifth Avenue, New York, NY 10010
fiercereads.com

Our books may be purchased in bulk for promotional, educational, or business use. Please
contact your local bookseller or the Macmillan Corporate and Premium Sales Department at
(800) 221-7945 ext. 5442 or by email at MacmillanSpecialMarkets@macmillan.com.

Library of Congress Cataloging-in-Publication Data

Names: Savage, Kim, 1969– author.
Title: In her skin / Kim Savage.
Description: New York : Farrar, Straus and Giroux, 2018. | Summary: Jolene Chastain,
    a con artist since early childhood, assumes the identity of a girl who went missing
    years before and weaves a new life of deception with a wealthy Boston family.
Identifiers: LCCN 2017021469 (print) | ISBN 978-1-250-29466-1 (paperback) |
    ISBN 978-0-374-30801-8 (ebook)
Subjects: | CYAC: Impersonation—Fiction. | Swindlers and swindling—Fiction. |
    Missing persons—Fiction. | Family life—Massachusetts—Boston—Fiction. |
    Boston (Mass.)—Fiction.
Classification: LCC PZ7.1.S27 In 2018 (print) | DDC [Fic]—dc23
LC record available at https://lccn.loc.gov/2017021469

Originally published in the United States by Farrar Straus Giroux
First Square Fish edition, 2019
Book designed by Elizabeth H. Clark
Square Fish logo designed by Filomena Tuosto

1   3   5   7   9   10   8   6   4   2

LEXILE: 840L

For my sparkler, Lila, who knows exactly who she is,

and for Dad. I feel your sunshine on my shoulders, still.

PART I
VIVI

I was seven the first time Momma taught me how to be someone else.

Sitting cross-legged on the street holding a coffee can for change, I'd listen as she'd tell me to remember how in a past life, I was blind. Straightaway, my eyes would blur, and sure as rain that can would be stuffed with bills by the end of the day. Momma said I had a thousand experiences to tap, because I'd passed through this world many times before. It was just a case of remembering.

Momma taught me other things. Like how flipping the pillow helps you sleep cool when the electricity gets turned off. How pretending every visit to a soup kitchen is your first gets you an extra roll. How saying a thing three times makes it so. How Happy Meals from the trash always contain perfectly good fries. How the only safe people are women with babies. How if something bad ever happened to her, I should run as far away from Immokalee as I could.

So I did.

Looking back, I guess I was still in shock from Momma getting killed, though her boyfriends beating her was as regular as the sun rising. I wasn't quite right in my head. On the bus from Florida, the only seat left was next to me. When a girl close to my age, about fourteen, took it, she put so much space between us you'd think I was day-old fish. She was clean around the fingernails where I wasn't, and had a neat little suitcase that someone had packed for her, and hardware on her teeth that meant someone with money cared enough to fix them. She told the driver loud that she was headed back to her family in Boston. A momma and a daddy, and a sister so close in age they were called twins. The driver said he'd be sure to watch over her, be her family till he got her back there safe.

If I was feeling like myself, I would have taught that girl not to scoot away from me. Regular Jolene Chastain would have reached over and pinched that girl's milk-thigh hard as she could. But I was in shock from seeing Momma the way a girl should never see her momma. So I went to a different place. I leaned back and pretended I was that girl, that her dimpled bare knees and the suitcase on the bus floor were mine, and that I was going back home to my momma, daddy, and a sister besides. It was a pretty thought. I started to think maybe it was a sign, me seeing that girl, and that my destiny in this life was to have that family.

Maybe if I hadn't seen that girl, heard her plans and started imagining they were mine, I wouldn't have had such a hard time on the street this last year. Living in Tent City is the closest I've come to having family, but Tent City is not my home. Here in the Boston Public Library I see lots of families, real ones that keep you clean and clothed and won't steal your shoes if you leave them outside your tent at night. So it's time to move on, and to that end, as they say, I have decided to mug you and become you.

You haven't noticed me watching. Here, in the library, I look like any other girl our age, even though the children's librarian with one brown tooth knows I'm homeless, performing my daily self-directed study: our private joke. A lot of us come here—the boy with the baby arm, the mutterer, the junkie in her stained hoodie—but I look the youngest. We're not afraid of getting tossed because we know the librarian is an easy mark, like most people who work with children. The teachers, the shelter counselors, the parole officers: their fatal flaw is that they only want to trust and be trusted.

But back to you. Your earring sparkles under the lights every time you brush your hair behind your ear. Earrings are hard—there will be screams, blood—but I'll come from behind, a quick yank on both ears at the same time: gone. Your earrings will be gone, and I'll be gone, and you'll never see me coming, you're so lost in that copy of *The Complete Poems of Emily Dickinson* propped beside your silver laptop in your tiny carrel, and you keep smelling the spine, honey hair sweeping over, nose to the page. You have a pink mark where your knee folds and I can tell you wish you could live inside that carrel like I already do, walls blocking out everything not in that book.

For the record, I would like to be a book nerd. I pretend to be, among these books, but I could never read them all. In Immokalee, I'd steal books from the Books for Africa bin at the dump: little-kid Golden Books with hard spines; cheesy, shiny-covered mysteries; classics with USED stickers on them from college bookstores. Sometimes I'd find poetry books, coffee rings on the covers. Like you, poetry is my favorite, because poems are like magic spells, and Momma taught me that words set in certain ways bring luck. I know we're connected, though anyone looking at us would say you are the un-me—a shiny girl who's never felt her mother's boyfriend brush up against her, never devoured a dirty lollipop dropped by a kid in the park, never slept in a bus terminal with a knife under her thigh for protection—you are me, just like me. So I wait until you go to the bathroom (with your computer, but not your wallet that fell off your lap the third time you crossed your overlong legs in that pleated skirt). I scan the room for Brown Tooth, and when I'm sure it's clear, I snag my score.

To become you, I need your social security number and a birthday. All your wallet contains is one black credit card that reads Henry Lovecraft and a school ID. I tuck the credit card in my sock and lean into the carrel, cupping your ID in my hands, which stink like something bad inside me is seeping out. I try to stay clean. It's easy not to look like a street kid if you're halfway clean, but the soap dispenser in the girls' room has been empty for days.

TEMPLE LOVECRAFT, the ID reads.

"Temple Lovecraft," I mouth.

You frown in the picture. Badass, with your chin tipped up. You love Emily Dickinson but you hate school. Why do you hate school? Because you go to a la-di-da all-girls school in the city when you'd rather be—where? You come here every day. You get off on poetry. You're coddled, fed. Yet you're empty. It's rare I can't figure out another person's wants and needs. It's how I live. You are worthy of study. But are you worthy of stealing? I flip the ID over. Trapped under plastic, your cheek can't feel me drag my thumb over it slowly.

"Fifteen minutes until closing," Brown Tooth shouts. She doesn't aim this toward Baby Arm, or Muttermouth, or Hoodie, just me, because she worries about me. Wants me warned before I get turned out onto the street for the night. I lean back in my chair and nod to Brown Tooth. To speak would encourage Brown Tooth, and I have ten minutes left to mine the Interwebs for your address, where I will paw through your trash for helpful digits. I've got five more minutes to write the note I will leave in my carrel, tacked with gum to the inside of the green lampshade for Wolf to find. He'll look for me here, after I leave him asleep in our tent tonight, headed for my new life as Temple Lovecraft.

Don't think about Wolf. Same way you don't think about Momma.

Wolf's better off without you. Better off without you. Better off.

Saying a thing three times makes it so.

I rush across the hall to a computer station and type *Temple Lovecraft*. I have to be quick, because they'll shut down the servers soon, and I'd like to drop this wallet back under your chair before you return from your visit to the girls' room.

Oh. Look.

It's you! The daughter of Henry and Clarissa Love-craft of Boston's Back Bay in a tasteful dress standing next to your catalog parents at an event called Charity Begins at Home, where lots of other kids and their rich parents are in *The Boston Globe*'s People and Places section. And Dad is the owner of Lovecraft Construction, the name on the crane that rises against the twinkly Boston sky-line that Wolf and me see from our tent flap every night. In one panting article after another, you're named a United States Presidential Scholar and a National Merit Scholar. You won the National French Contest, the Hamilton Award, and the World Scholar's Cup, which has nothing to do with soccer. Not that you aren't sporty. You rank first on the national girls' varsity fencing team. You're musical, too: first cello in the Boston Youth Con-servatory and, when you were younger, you were a child opera singer featured on *America's Got Talent* until "vocal nodules ended a promising career." To keep up with all this stuff, you told a reporter you pull all-nighters to study "on a regular basis." The reporter ends her article by tell-ing us "Pinned to her bedroom wall is a quotation from

Oliver Cromwell: 'He who stops being better, stops being good.'"

You dazzle me, Temple Lovecraft. But I still need your address. I type *Lovecraft* alongside *Back Bay apartment* and . . . what's this?

NINE-YEAR-OLD GOES MISSING FROM PROMINENT LOCAL DEVELOPER'S HOME

By Stephanie Ebbert | BOSTON GLOBE MAY 23, 2010

Boston—A nine-year-old girl has gone missing from a Back Bay apartment as her playmate's parents sat dining several feet away.

Vivienne Weir, the daughter of Travis and Marie Weir, was last seen in the brownstone town house owned by Boston developer Henry Lovecraft and his wife, Clarissa. The Lovecrafts were seated in the outdoor section of Restaurant Chloe, which is attached to their home on Commonwealth Avenue, where they say they left Weir and their daughter alone watching a television show around seven p.m.

Abductions with parents in proximity are rare but not unheard of, making the case reminiscent of the 2007 disappearance of four-year-old Madeleine McCann, the British girl who vanished from her hotel room at a resort in Portugal while her parents dined fifty yards away.

Below the article is a photo of a girl taken from the waist up. The back of her head nestles against the chest of a woman who is cropped out, except for her chin, arms that cross the girl in a hug, and dark curls that spill onto the girl's shoulder. The girl's own hair is the color of butter, and she has big square teeth. Her eyes make happy half-moons, like someone she loved said "Smile!" and she did, because she had reasons to. I settle on the woman's arms. They hug the girl so hard, the front of her bathing suit puckers.

My breath burns.

The want I feel for those phantom arms could shatter the screen. Make it pop, sizzle, and die. Make the shelves shake and the books tumble down. The want's like with the girl on the bus, but it wasn't useful then, and it's not useful right now.

Stealing Temple Lovecraft's identity will get me money. It will get me off the street. But it won't get me those arms.

I type *Vivienne Weir*. The next story reads fast.

PLANE CRASH OFF NANTUCKET KILLS
BOSTON COUPLE

By Julie Dalton | BOSTON GLOBE July 2, 2011

Nantucket, Massachusetts—Fog is believed to be the cause of a small plane crash off the coast of Nantucket Friday evening. The passengers, Travis and Marie Weir of Boston, are presumed dead. The Weirs are the parents of nine-year-old Vivienne Weir, who went missing in May 2010.

I did not see that coming.

Which is rare.

I tab back to the photo of Vivienne in the sun. The Weirs are dead and they were vain. Instead of giving the newspaper a useful photo of their daughter, they gave the newspaper a pretty one, one that showed them on some fancy vacation, tanned and happy. My hand curls around my neck, dirty hair brushing my knuckles—hair that might have been lighter once. Vivienne's smile is sweet and her cheeks are round, but teeth rot and faces drop with misery. Behind the basic pretty that care affords Vivienne is plain, and plain can morph into anything.

The loudspeaker booms: "The library will close in five minutes."

When dead, vain parents plunge into the sea, they leave behind loving relatives to care for their child. Loving relatives who might not look for that mole, this scar, that overlapping tooth.

"Please bring any items to be checked out to the circulation desk."

Wallet! I scramble off my seat and run back to the carrels. Yours is empty, the pull-chain on the banker's lamp swinging, your chair pushed far beneath the desk. Temple Lovecraft is slippery. Temple Lovecraft is gone. But what if Vivienne Weir was back?

I am Vivienne Weir. I am Vivienne Weir. I am Vivienne. Three times makes it so.

. . . . .

The back rooms of Precinct 1440 smell of burnt coffee and desperation. It is loud and disorganized enough that someone left a picture of an age-progressed Vivienne Weir tacked right on the wall.

An expression leaves a mark on your face if you repeat it enough. The forensic artist knows this, because in the picture on the right, sixteen-year-old Vivienne Weir has teeny wrinkles beside the bridge of her nose. In the actual photo of nine-year-old Vivienne Weir on the left—the last one taken before she disappeared, the same one in the newspaper—her face is in the act of making those exact lines. I shake my hair around my face (people in shock do this) and lean forward, practicing that exploding smile over and over again.

The wrinkled lap of a skirt appears inches from my nose. I lose Vivienne's smile and raise my chin slowly.

"Here's your Coke," the police social worker says, slipping back into her chair across from me. "Now, can you tell us anything else?"

I ignore the sweaty Coke, look her full in the face, and say for the third time, "My name is Vivienne."

Police social workers like Ginny have terrible jobs. They aren't real shrinks and they aren't cops and they get dragged out of bed in the middle of the night to work with what the cops don't want to work with. I met one the time Momma and me got caught in a sting. Her name was Reva and she sipped the same Styrofoam cup of tea for hours and her breath smelled like nail polish remover and she wanted to "reach" me the same way Ginny wants to reach me now. But I don't need to be reached, I need to be off the streets and nestled in with a brand-new family, and Ginny's going to help me whether she knows it or not.

Ginny is today's mark.

I tuck my mouth and eye the half-eaten doughnut sitting between us, bleeding jelly. Vivienne wouldn't have gnawed at it the way I did, even if she was semi-starved. She'd take baby bites, because a jelly doughnut was considered a sometimes-treat to her instead of enough sugar and fat to live off for three days.

"No matter what you say, nobody will be upset with you. We need anything you can remember about your abductor," Ginny says, pinching her forehead between thumb and forefinger. "For your own safety."

She's getting tired but she won't give up, this Ginny, because Ginny is good at her job. It's the only thing in her life she is good at. I need to be her win. Two cops drag in an old hooker by her sleeves. She's screaming about being profiled even though she is very clearly a hooker, and her voice is on the same wavelength as Momma's, hoarse from cigarettes and stomach acid. When she cuts her way around us, jerking and yelling, Ginny doesn't blink, but I do, because I hear Momma's voice, smell her Pall Malls and cherry Tums.

The hooker's voice is a sign. It's Momma telling me this plan is a good one.

Ginny ignores the hooker. "Consider the other girls he could abduct," she presses. "These kinds of criminals don't quit until they get caught."

Actually, Ginny, these kinds of criminals get caught all the time, and then they get sprung, and then they take out getting caught on their girlfriends. Sometimes, they kill them.

"I told you. I don't remember anything."

Ginny rises and I follow her into a conference room with buzzy fluorescent lights, because Vivienne would follow an adult. Ginny settles into a new seat in the new room. I expect the suspicious detective named Curley who is assigned my case to take her place, to play Bad Cop, because that's the only reason they bring you to a separate room. It's like pushing a reset button. Only Ginny didn't get the memo and launches in one more time.

"Seven years held by the same man. That's a long time not to remember anything about him."

Ginny's thinking I have Stockholm syndrome and I'm thinking I have Can't-Make-It-Up-Fast-Enough syndrome and people like Ginny and the librarian and Reva are all the same. When Ginny goes home at night to her sad cats in her sad condo, she feels her job rewards her, though she probably reuses tea bags and drives an eleven-year-old Corolla with a suction-cupped GPS and charges groceries on her credit card. I don't feel bad for her, but I do need to move things along, and you'd think she'd be getting antsy since that network TV show calling her name starts ninety minutes from now.

I exhale slowly.

"The last thing I remember is someone pressing a smelly cloth over my nose and mouth. I woke up in a shed. And I stayed there. For a long time. I don't know how long. The man fed me. Food you get from drive-throughs and gas stations. He hit me. A lot. I escaped through a rotted plank that I carved away at with a nail, every day. The next thing I remember, I'm here, on the steps of the police station." I let my chin fall in dramatic silence.

After a respectful pause, Ginny whispers, "Thank you, Vivienne."

I smile into my neck, because she called me Vivienne.

"I'd like to see my mother now," I whisper. It sounds weird coming from my mouth, because my mother is dead.

As I remember this, my eyes fill with tears.

"Sweetheart," Ginny says, "I know this must be very

hard. I'm going to make a promise to you. I'm going to make sure that you get every resource you need. A therapist to talk to. Maybe a stress animal. Do you know what those are? They're pets specially trained to sense when your anxiety level goes up, and when they do, they give you comfort—"

"No."

Ginny's eyelids shoot up. "No you don't know?"

"No I don't want one." What kid doesn't want a pet? Stupid Jo. "I mean, mostly, I'd like another doughnut." I need Ginny to lay off and give me some time to work on the shed thing. I'll have to soft-pedal Vivi's lockup during those seven years. At a certain point, it's easier for everyone, even a sourpuss like Curley, to think of a missing kid as dead than alive, because they don't have to imagine what she must have gone through. We'll talk about "moving on" and not giving my perpetrator one more minute of my life. Fuzzy details will be welcome. Therapy appointments will be made. A foster family will be assigned, as will a pet, funded by the Commonwealth of Massachusetts. Ginny might be mine, but if the cops don't buy that I'm Missing Vivi, I'll know right away by their headshaking disappointment, by how they back away a little. In that case, I'll ask to go pee for the second time, in the bathroom where I've loosened the screws on the window grate. The back alley leads to the YMCA, and farther, down Huntington Avenue, where I can get lost in the sea of college kids from Northeastern.

Detective Curley pops his head in and gives Ginny a questioning look.

Ginny nods solemnly. "Make the call."

I try to sound excited. "You're calling my parents?"

The lines around Ginny's mouth deepen and she looks away. I fake squinty confusion. Rule number one Momma taught me: stay in character, even when no one's looking.

"Vivi," Ginny says, leaning forward and grasping my hand; it's the first time she's called me Vivi, and touching me is not police social worker protocol, since you don't touch the Maybe Diddled. She's going off book, which means she's stuck. There are no guidelines for magically reappearing orphaned dead girls, at least not ones she's read. "There was an accident. Your father was piloting a small chartered plane to Nantucket, like he sometimes did. And there was weather, and he and your mother—their plane, that is—crashed. And they are no longer. I'm terribly sorry."

There's something crazy and wrong about this woman

acting like a plane crash is the worst possible thing that can kill your mother. It's the best possible thing that can happen, Ginny! Having your mother plunged into the Atlantic is better than having your mother's cheekbones caved in by a fist. And Vivi never had to see any of it, and . . .

And Ginny's hugging me. She smells like lilac powder and BO, and I heave once for effect and peek over her arm to the floor where her bag gapes. Inside is a fat file, probably about Vivi. A fat file I can use.

I peel away gently.

"Your parents never gave up hope that they would find you," Ginny says with feeling. "Before they died, they arranged for your neighbors to get custody of you if anything happened to them. Do you remember Mr. and Mrs. Lovecraft?"

I look up, blinking back tears. "The Lovecrafts?"

She doesn't miss a beat. "You remember! The parents of your friend. Her name is Temple. They live two doors down."

I choke.

Ginny does a sad puppy face. "I'm deeply sorry."

I nod hard. "I know you are."

She looks at me strangely, like I am a wondrous creature,

like I know she is awkward and I am making this easy on her and Ginny is hugging me again.

"How soon until they get here?" I squeak.

An angry rap on the half-open door. Detective Curley hears Ginny and wants her to stop talking to me. She's giving away too much information, he thinks, but he's already lost this one: Ginny's on my side. I'm the success story that makes Ginny satisfied with a job that pays her less in one year than Momma made in one month of check kiting. And Temple Lovecraft, library Temple, fascinating Temple, is my new sister.

Then the detective and Ginny do the unexpected. They leave me sitting alone for what only feels like hours because the conference room has no clock. There is someone on the other side of this who is researching child-welfare laws and checking wills and making phone calls and it feels out of my control. They leave me with the soggy cup of Coke and a stained travel pillow from Ginny's car where I rest my cheek, and I want to think about Temple but instead I am thinking about Wolf and our tent, and it seems like a million years ago since last night, when I lay awake staring through the half-light at his delicate chin, a chin not made for lives like ours, and the shadows that line his nose, thinking about how his beauty will always be his enemy, attracting the paying men he doesn't want to attract, and knowing, traitor that I am, that it would be our last night. Wolf and I have been together since we arrived at Tent City on the same day, me helping him survive, him helping me not get raped by attaching himself to me. He's older than me, but younger in the head. He is bored by the books I crave. Still, he doesn't mind my days spent at the library, when by rights I should be helping him panhandle and Dumpster dive and carry water up from the rain barrels instead of reading. Wolf accepts my cravings and I accept his, which leave raised red rings on his thighs, because cutting on the street means infection, but burning with cigarettes kills germs. And in this way, we work. Wolf is the closest I've come to having a boyfriend, but one boyfriend does not a family make.

And this is where I leave him.

. . . . .

Remembering past lives isn't my only skill. Long ago, I learned I was good at using the ones right in front of me. Momma had a name for it: said I was an intuit.

Every time I switched schools, to avoid getting teased for my backwater accent or my short pants, I'd pick a certain girl—the girl whose laugh could leave you bleeding, the one who moved other kids around like chess pieces, the one teachers let get away with murder. I couldn't copy clothes, or the smell of clean scalp, or a hard little chin. But I'd get good at the cool rhythm of her speech, her shuffle walk, her nonchalance. Eventually, it wasn't enough to be on the outside: I wanted in. So I decided things. I thought she might be a late sleeper. That she liked salty over sweet. She tanned easy, and had a stripe of white underneath the woven bracelet on her ankle. The lines around both of us dissolved until I was looking through her eyes, and those eyes were fierce slits. When one of Momma's boyfriends would block my way, I'd push past him, sweeping my shoulder like he'd shed something bad. If Momma limped from a kidney punch, I spat into the boyfriend's scrambled eggs and coolly watched him eat. Momma's scams were just games, games that I played along with because I wanted to, and I could stop at any time.

Inside the girl's ferocity, I hardened.

· · · · ·

I must have slept. New faces crowd the door. In Tent City, cheeks thicken from weather and booze, and eyes flicker. These faces are strange in their delicateness and their concern. I pull my dirty sleeves over my hands and slip down in my chair. Under the stares of these people, everything feels wrong: the distance between my eyes, the shape of my lips, the width of my pelvis. The excitement of a few hours ago has evaporated and I am scared. I don't have Vivi in the flesh to observe, to know what she would do next.

Momma would tell me to remember when I was a soldier returning from battle. You've seen and done unspeakable things, she'd say, and now you are home.

I make my cheeks sag with weariness and my eyes light up with relief. It's not the easiest combination. Momma would be proud.

A woman takes a careful step into the room, with Ginny and the detective behind. The woman's face is unlined and her hair thins at the temples—she wouldn't like that I notice this, is self-conscious about it—and her raincoat is tied at the waist, a plaid pattern that looks frumpy but means the coat is expensive and worth stealing. She has pale, wide-spaced eyes and a nose turned down at the tip, and the same hair as Temple, light-filled syrup, only shorter. Her mouth is tight, but there is movement underneath, like she's turning thoughts over in it and finds them sour. She pinches her throat between two fingers, leaving pink. Taken together, these are not good signs. But I shouldn't assume this is going to be easy. Hadn't assumed it. Won't assume it.

A man comes behind her, more obviously beautiful. Not how Wolf is beautiful, which is the kind of beautiful you look away from. The kind that gets carved and eaten by hungry men. This is the man who does the eating. This man is ravenous, a man whose shoulders dip and rise as he walks, who uses his whole long body to speak, though he hasn't yet. He has a neat new beard because it is trendy, and it will be gone next week. I can see his arms through the sports coat, and the coat has been cut to do that very thing. The kind of man who could bang the babysitter but maybe doesn't. Not because of what she lacks—they are not equals, these two—but because it is beneath him.

Ginny clears her throat. No one looks at her. She lumps her way forward, graceless against these people. Detective Curley hangs back, watching.

"Vivi?" Ginny asks. Not a statement but a question. My only ally in the room maybe isn't an ally.

This was a mistake. I glance into the hallway, toward the bathroom: my escape to Huntington Avenue.

"Vivi," Ginny repeats.

My head snaps. "Yes?"

Detective Curley pushes into the room, holding up his hand to silence Ginny. He wants to see my face. He wants recognition; proof. Because Vivi was nine, and Vivi would remember these people. But I'm not going to give the detective a full reckoning, because I've been through a lot in that shed. Enough to wipe a memory near clean.

I blink as if through fog.

The woman comes forward in a sweeping rush. "Vivi!" she says, breathy, and crouches beside me, her forehead wrinkling in happy layers. Excitement works for her: she is prettified. The man joins her, still standing; this is not a man who crouches. She searches my face as I search hers. It feels like a violation, those pale eyes over my face, but to look away is suspicious.

"Mrs. Lovecraft . . . ," Ginny starts.

Mrs. Lovecraft's eyes are not for Ginny. "May I touch your hand?" she asks.

"Mrs. Lovecraft, we really don't know the extent to which—the trauma . . . ," Ginny falters. Ginny is doing a terrible job setting boundaries, and the detective is getting madder. Even I'm mad at Ginny. Because none of this is by the book. It's strange, to feel like a prize, a rare thing that a rich woman wants to touch.

I nod.

Mrs. Lovecraft places her cool hand on mine. "You are Vivi," she whispers.

Mr. Lovecraft turns to the detective. "We'd like to take her home now."

Detective Curley gets his back up. "That is not happening. We need to take statements. A rape k—"

"Medical exam," Ginny corrects.

I look to Mrs. Lovecraft wildly. "I don't want anyone touching me."

She looks to her husband, begging.

He leans toward the detective. "The Weirs' will states that we are Vivienne's legal guardians. There is no reason we can't just take her home right now." He slips a white card into the detective's hand. "That's my attorney's number, if there are any questions."

"Leaving so soon may not be in the best interests of the child," Ginny warns. "There will be therapy. Grief counseling."

"Mr. and Mrs. Lovecraft, we don't yet have a full statement from the victim. There's a criminal out there to find," Detective Curley says.

I look only at Mrs. Lovecraft. Mr. Lovecraft has hardly looked at me. I should be relieved by this, since I don't trust men much, but it pokes at me, messes with my performance. I refocus on her.

"I want to leave this place," I beg.

Mrs. Lovecraft rises. "You said our coming here was for the purpose of identification. This is Vivienne Weir. She was like a daughter to me." She turns her smile on me. "I would know her anywhere."

Ginny covers her mouth hard, thinking. She wants this win badly. Mr. Lovecraft and the detective glare at each other. Finally, Ginny drops her arms and turns to the detective. "It's late. It wouldn't hurt anyone if Vivienne went home with the Lovecrafts tonight and came back tomorrow. The police can take their statements then, and I can provide therapy referrals. Phone numbers, names. A plan. Will that work?"

I look at Mr. Lovecraft full-on for the first time. He gazes at his wife and they smile at each other, not with their mouths but with their eyes. I won't be coming back here tomorrow, and I am grinning like a dead pig in sunshine, which is inappropriate, so I stop.

Mrs. Lovecraft takes a long look at my unshowered-ness, at my body pouring from my too-small sweatshirt and ripped leggings, the ones I stole from the tent of a younger girl. I am dirt and sex, too, and maybe that's why Mr. Lovecraft hasn't looked at me yet, though I don't think so.

The station buzzes, an angry vibe, charged by the fact that we are leaving together, which is against the rules. Suited detectives and uniformed cops and the dispatcher who works the phone and even the hooker stare. Mr. Lovecraft is a tall glass of water, and it feels good to walk alongside him. We step outside into the night to their car at the curb. As I sink into the backseat of their huge SUV with its tinted windows, I almost don't care what they do to me. Because the possibility that these people are perverts is low, but it's still a possibility.

Mrs. Lovecraft looks over her seat. "Are you tired, Vivi?"

I nod. The relief of being out of the police station is overpowering. I try to say "very" but it gets caught in my throat.

Mrs. Lovecraft's face bunches up. "We don't need to talk now. You should rest. Go ahead, lie down in the backseat. We don't mind if you don't wear your seat belt."

As if the worst thing that could happen to a girl who was held captive in a man's backyard for seven years is getting whiplash in a car accident. I'm starting to see these announcements as the habits of people who live with roofs over their heads—pointing out the mildly unsafe to keep away the real horrors. The Lovecrafts are halfway right. Words have power, but you have to use them the correct way.

My family. My family. Mine.

Mr. Lovecraft presses a lit screen and fills the car with soft music. I have never seen Boston through the inside of a car window, and it's a different city. People in light jackets huddle and rush and laugh, the women in shoes made from expensive animals walking with men who look like they smell good when the women lean in. The store displays are lit jewel boxes, and the sidewalks are even and clean, and inside this car you can't smell the garbage and the pee, the exhaust and the sausages. As we turn off Newbury Street and take another right onto Commonwealth Avenue, the street is lined with newly budded trees strung with white lights. This is the Lovecrafts' city, and it glows. I went to a buffet restaurant once and this is like that: food for miles, so many things to choose from, and I want to gobble it up.

I touch the window.

Mr. Lovecraft looks back. "Don't worry about going

back to the station. We would never put you through remembering. This is a new start for you, Vivi."

They murmur in the front seat, their words watering as I drift again. I catch the name Temple a lot, and there is worry in their voices, worry that relates to newspaper reporters and people who remember our case, but the city is beautiful tonight, because Henry and Clarissa Lovecraft are going to take care of me.

We park a few blocks away from the Lovecrafts' brownstone. Mrs. Lovecraft rubs her thin arms as we walk. "There's nothing prettier than May in Boston," she says. "When the dogwoods bloom. Though they hardly last." We stop as Mr. Lovecraft slips off his scarf and wraps it around her neck. She lifts her hair. They don't speak: this is a practiced act, an expected one.

"What Clarissa's saying," he says, tweaking the scarf, "is that you picked the perfect time to come back to us."

I smile weakly at the ground. I am from Boston. I am supposed to know that this city is pretty in May but pretty doesn't last. On the street corner ahead, laughter trails from a group leaving a restaurant. This is *the* restaurant next door, maybe not exactly the same restaurant where the Lovecrafts sat when Vivi disappeared, but the same spot. Which seems totally wrong, now that I'm on this well-lit sidewalk on Commonwealth Avenue. This is a busy part of the city, a neighborhood for sure, but still busy, and suddenly I want to know the details of Vivi's abduction. How did the kidnapper get in? How did he escape with Vivi without anyone seeing? Is there an alley in the back? How did Temple not hear anything?

Mr. Lovecraft cups my shoulder and I jump.

"I didn't mean to startle you," he says. "We're here."

"Right," I say, stopping at a set of stairs leading to two huge front doors. I gaze up; the town house is three stories high. I start to ask if they live in this whole thing, but stop myself, because Vivi would know.

A man meets us in the marbled entrance. They introduce him as Slade. Slade is at least six foot three and over two hundred pounds, fit but puffy, wearing a jacket and jeans, and that jacket indoors in May means he's packing heat. The skin under Slade's eyes is gray, and he makes a meaty-lipped smile while he tries not to look at my chest. I wonder if those under-eye circles mean he stays up late watching porn.

Mr. Lovecraft explains that Slade "spent time in Iraq" and "recently transitioned" into "private client security."

Slade tongues his gum into his cheek. "Nice meeting you, Miss Weir," he says as he holds out his hand. I shake it limply.

"We've used security professionals like Slade for the last few years. Just a precaution. A lot of folks in our circles do it," Mr. Lovecraft says.

"In our circles" means income bracket and "the last few years" means since Vivi vanished, and who exactly are the Lovecrafts taking precautions against? Seven years later, are they still afraid someone will climb through a window and steal you?

Slade waits for the Lovecrafts to tell him what to do next, but the Lovecrafts are looking at me like I'm a fish in a tank again, and maybe they've forgotten him already. When Slade shifts and makes a small noise, Mr. Lovecraft comes to.

"That'll be all for now, Slade."

"I'll be in my room, then," Slade says, bounding up a set of stairs, and do all rich people have sleep-in bodyguards? We enter a room with a crystal chandelier dripping from a ceiling painted blue. Not the endless blue of the Florida sky, but mixed with streams of clouds. Where the walls meet the ceiling is trim like frosting, with fruit and baby angels in the corners made of the same white stuff, four of them, mouths open like they're screaming.

"We've redecorated a bit," Mrs. Lovecraft says, spinning as if she's new to it herself. It's hard not to gape at this house I am supposed to know, even if it is changed.

"Technically, *she* redecorated," Mr. Lovecraft says, squeezing his wife's skinny shoulders. They touch each other a lot. Momma's boyfriends touched Momma a lot, and me sometimes, too, but I don't remember liking it. Mostly it made me think about them bloated, dead on the ground.

"This atrium has become my favorite room in the whole house," Mrs. Lovecraft says about this room that is the center of everything. In one direction, a polished stair rail leads up; in another is a kitchen with lights over a shiny island, and in another, a cozy room with a fireplace and a standing mirror with a curlicue gold frame and a puckered turquoise couch. In the fourth direction is an office with a desk in the middle and a file cabinet beside it. The desk faces a barred window looking out onto that same restaurant. I wonder if it's hard for whoever sits at that desk to look at that restaurant every day.

"It's been a long day for you. You must want a bath," she says.

I stiffen; maybe they are perverts. More importantly, do I care?

My weirdness registers with her. She looks at Mr. Lovecraft again worriedly before saying, "Or not."

Mr. Lovecraft moves about the first floor, pulling closed

the heavy drapes, shutting out the city, the restaurant, and the night. I like the way he gives us space when we're talking about me bathing. It's probably just good breeding, but it feels like respect.

"No, it's fine," I say. "You want me clean. It's okay."

She looks at me, puzzled. "That is, if you want to be clean. It's up to you." She looks over my body gently, imagining bad touches, and lowers her voice. "We can't begin to understand what you've been through these last years. We know it's going to take time for you to acclimate. That's why we decided it would be better to wait for you to see Temple."

"You sent her away?" I ask.

"No," Mrs. Lovecraft says, looking up at the staircase as she says it. "She's here. We just thought it would be a good idea to give you some space tonight. It's late, and you should clean up and get some sleep."

"I just thought I'd meet everyone, you know, tonight."

"The truth is, this is hard on Temple, too. Not that she's not thrilled that you're back. We're all thrilled. Your return changes our lives. The papers will want your story—'The Return of Vivienne Weir'—so we'll have to manage that. You'll be going to school, sharing our home. It's a lot for a teenager to adjust to."

"We were friends," I say. "Sisters, basically."

"Well, of course. But that was when you were nine. Temple is sixteen. And you're—"

"Sixteen," I say.

"Sixteen. Time has passed. I'm sure you'll be close again, but it might take a little while."

From the stairs comes a creak.

We snap our heads. Temple Lovecraft is perched on the stairs, hugging her sharp flannel knees.

"Darling!" Mr. Lovecraft exclaims. "Come down and say hello to Vivi."

You release your knees, unfold your long body, and walk down the stairs slow, slower than I know you have energy for, because I watched you before you knew I was watching. Your feet are bare and white, and bones rise under your camisole straps forming diamond caves. You stand in your pale cami and your hair braided at the temples (Temple!) and tucked behind your ears, so close I can see the pin-dot holes where the diamonds were and smell the black licorice you just ate on your breath. Your eyes start at the top of my head and work their way down: the crown of my forehead, eyes. A flick between both ears, down the nose and settling on my mouth. I twitch. To my chin and down my neck: chest, hands, waist, and knees, every part examined. I am not safe under plastic and your eyes are not my clumsy thumb. Years with Momma's boyfriends have hardened me to stares, but by the time you get to my feet, my heart is pounding so loud I am sure you can hear it.

Do you know me?

In an instant, your mother is at my side. "You're thinking it's a miracle, aren't you?" she says, hugging you at the shoulder.

You only look at me.

"Temple," Mr. Lovecraft says. "Your mother asked you a question."

Mrs. Lovecraft waves it off. "Vivi's been through so much. We have time to catch up. For now, sleep."

Your eyes flash over me one last time, wary. You aren't sure. I tell myself it's not that my eyes are blue where Vivi's were gray. It's not that my left front tooth crosses over my right, where Vivi's teeth were strong and straight. It's that you don't want Vivi back. And I don't blame you. Vivi was your friend from third grade. You had third-grade things in common: boy bands and glitter nail polish and diaries. I'm going to have to win you over as Vivi, when Jolene Chastain would talk to you about Emily Dickinson and books with coffee rings on their covers and in a book, this is called irony.

Of course you're iffy about me. You're Miss Number One Everything. Vivi's return takes the spotlight off you. Where I spent half my life trying to become invisible from Momma's boyfriends and the cops, you've spent sixteen years as the center of boot-licking admiration. You and Vivi may have history, but Vivi's reappearance could make your whole life go sideways. So yes, it is to be expected that you won't embrace me.

Yet.

With a swish of flannel and hair you are gone. Mrs. Lovecraft puts her arm around my shoulder, just as she did with you, and I show her I like it with a weak smile.

"You're going to have to excuse Temple," she says, steering me toward the stairs. "She has so many questions. In time, she'll adjust to your being back."

"Where are we going?" I ask.

"To your room," Mrs. Lovecraft says.

I never go to sleep this early. The less you sleep in Tent City, the less you lose. As if she reads my mind, she says, "Do you think you'll be able to sleep? I imagine it must be hard to quiet your mind."

Ahh. Bad Shed Thoughts. I haven't fully considered the explanations Vivi's kidnapping will provide, from avoiding eye contact to keeping my clothes on to my crappy dental hygiene.

"So hard," I murmur.

"I think I have something that will help," she says, leading me up the stairs. Behind us, Mr. Lovecraft slips into his office and slides the pocket door closed. She leads me to the second floor, where a pretty window seat looks out across the Commonwealth Avenue mall to the Charles and the blinking lights of Cambridge. She points out the bedroom and bathroom she shares with Mr. Lovecraft, and a third room, its door shut.

"This is where Slade stays," she explains. "The surveillance we employ him for requires him to stay awake through the night and sleep during the day. I don't want you to be surprised if you hear anything at odd hours."

"So, he protects the family while you sleep?"

"That's right."

The house gets narrow as we climb to the third floor, where, again, there are three doors. One leads to what will be my room, which is wallpapered royal blue with tiny gold lilies and contains a dresser, a nightstand, and a four-poster bed fit for a princess. The covers are pulled back at the corner; underneath, the sheets are fresh-looking and tight. My body aches for that bed. The second door is yours, and it's shut. A tiny bathroom is behind the third, with a tub perched on claw feet and a tufted rug. There is old-fancy and old-crappy, and this is the first.

Mrs. Lovecraft feels for a plushy robe behind the door and hands it to me before twisting the gold faucet on. She straightens and digs her knuckles into her hips. I stare at the water pouring into the tub and I cannot get under that water fast enough.

"Do you need help getting undressed?" she asks, pitchy. She hopes I'll say no so she doesn't have to see the stories Vivi's naked body will tell her.

"I'm good."

"Then may I give you something to relax?"

I am a Popsicle on a summer day and Clarissa Lovecraft is the sun, and she is offering a soft, cool bed and hot water and now drugs, and I could make out with her, and where at first she was a woman who seemed less than her handsome husband, now she is a goddess, with her beginnings of a neck wattle and her noble beak-nose.

I nod hard.

She disappears and returns with two green pills. "Ativan. Perfectly safe if you don't make a habit of it." I want to tell her that if I didn't make it a habit in Tent City, where one out of two residents is stoned out of their mind, and if I didn't make it a habit in the years when Momma was using, I'm not going to make a habit of it in Back Bay.

I accept the pills and toss them back. She hands me a paper cup of water, but I've already swallowed. Smiling softly from the side of her mouth, she leads me back to the bedroom, where I am finally alone. As I drop another street kid's clothes, light bounces at the window. I pull on the robe, creep to the window, and look down. The story of Vivienne Weir's return is making the eleven o'clock news. A woman stands before the Lovecrafts' brownstone, holding a mic next to a News 5 truck with a spiral cable running up a pole. I shove the window up, sleeves flopping, and I hear her talking, but I can't make out her words over cars zooming to beat the light at the corner of Dartmouth and Commonwealth. With luck, the reporters will move on, and I will be embraced by this over-the-top house and the arms of my new well-groomed parents who ooze love and maybe you, Temple, will come to love me, too. The edges grow soft, and I hear the water running across the hall, and it's been a year since my baths didn't involve a restroom and mealy paper towels, and you can't pay for this kind of white noise. I tip-toe from my room. The Lovecrafts talk excitedly in their bedroom below, probably because they saw the news truck. I don't want to wake you, who, as the drug moves through my bloodstream, seem less threatened by me and more curious. Catlike. I slip into the steamy bathroom, shut the door with a soft click, drop my robe and close the faucet.

The water is heaven. Under these bubbles floats my own filth, but I don't care, because the bubbles smell like apples and I am good. I didn't know how tight my muscles were from sleeping on the cardboard box with the egg-crate pad, and then not sleeping, because some nights sleeping in Tent City isn't the best idea, some nights it's better for you to take turns sleeping while one person stays alert, listening—don't think about Wolf—and sometimes instead of sleeping, you both get up and walk until the sun rises, across town, to the Charles and along it. Above your head, the tree branches hold moonlight, and underneath, the path sparkles, and in the river, the light from Cambridge shimmers across black ripples— don't think about Wolf—and he rests his arm across your shoulder, and you wonder if he might be enough family for you.

I hold my breath and slip below the water. Let my hair bloom, let the warmth loosen my jaw. Don't choose to remember, Jolene. Choose to enjoy. After all, it may not last. Make the most of this tub and that bed and this drug.

A mean thought cuts through my Ativan haze, straight

out of a bad TV movie, of a hand holding my head under the water. I break the surface, gasping. I feel frantically for the robe on the floor and hold it over my face for a second, then two.

When I drop the robe, the door is cracked open.

I step from the tub covering my privates best I can and press the door shut with my elbow. Naked and dripping, I clear a circle in the mirror with my knuckles. Great black pupils. Slicked hair. Vulnerable. The girl in the mirror looks frightened by her own imagination. The girl in the mirror looks high. The girl in the mirror looks alone.

I smile close-mouthed. "Pervert," I whisper, in case the peeper was Slade and he's still lurking.

No matter. The Slades of the world do not concern me. I have a family, and that family has my back. I section the front of my wet hair and braid it, tucking the braids over my ears. Raise my shoulders until my collarbones make hollows. Lift my chin.

As Vivi's skin grows over mine, I will slip inside the Lovecrafts. I will slip inside the Lovecrafts. I will slip inside.

Now the girl in the mirror doesn't look so alone.

· · · · ·

In Immokalee, a wren flew into our house and got itself trapped. Momma and I tiptoed around it for days, leaving it seeds and a Dixie cup of water. Here, I am the wren. It's like the Lovecrafts think loud noises or too much bustling around might scare me away. I have been left nearly alone for my first full day, except for meals. Mr. Lovecraft talks on the phone in his office and Mrs. Lovecraft pretends to do things on her laptop in the kitchen, but her main job is running interference between you and me. The Lovecrafts have explained that "chilling" at home today is best, because we are "under a microscope." This feels true and not true. Besides the reporter last night, the street is full of rushing people who don't know us and don't care.

I shift to wake my legs, tucked underneath me in my hallway window seat high above Commonwealth Ave. The book on my lap crashes to the floor. The book is a prop, because Vivi would occupy herself by reading politely. I don't read, because reading would distract me from hearing you and your parents—our parents—whisper.

You laugh from below. Not a nice laugh: a "ha." A challenge.

More whispers; harsher tones. I grab a pillow and curl it into my chest.

I do not like this strange quiet. I would rather be thrust into acting like Vivi than waiting for something to go down. A juicy snore echoes from behind Slade's bedroom door, followed by a dreamy murmur that sounds like "more snacks."

I chuckle loudly.

Downstairs goes quiet. Stupid Jolene. Girls kept in sheds do not spontaneously laugh, particularly when they are alone. To disguise the laugh, I cough, loud and over the top.

Thirty seconds pass. A minute.

The whispers start again.

I exhale and press my hand against the glass. A homeless guy on the corner sells copies of *Spare Change News*. I'm not close enough to tell, but because I've been homeless I know that layers of street crust his pant cuffs. I know his work boots are heavy but not warm. I know his nose is chilled, because Boston gets cold when the sun drops. Momma always ran on the cold side, she said. I run my tongue over my crowded teeth and try not to think on Momma, because no good comes from thinking on the dead. Not Wolf neither, because no good comes from thinking on those you've left behind. There is only what lies ahead.

My eyes fill with dumb tears.

"Are you okay?"

I yelp.

You stand in the shadows on the landing, a plaid blanket wrapped against the wind that blows off the Charles. Your finger rises to your lips, dragging the blanket like a royal sleeve.

"Shh," you whisper.

"Why?" I whisper back.

"They don't want me up here."

I force myself to sit still and let you run your eyes across me again, over forehead and nose, out to the ear, mouth, and back to the eyes.

I can't help how I look, but there are other tricks. I lift my voice a shade and speak from my belly, so my words come from a softer place. "Your parents don't want you up here?"

"They want me to take it slow," you explain. "Give us both time to adjust."

I face the window, scrambling to get inside Vivi. "That's probably a good idea."

"They're worried. They always worry."

I crinkle my nose. "I know this turns your life upside down. And now I have to live here, which makes it doubly weird."

"It's definitely weird."

"I don't expect things to be the same. I'll never be the girl I was."

"I don't expect things to be the same either." You move closer to share my view. "They say I'm not supposed to ask you what it was like."

Thank you Mr. and Mrs. Lovecraft. "Yeah. I'm not really ready to talk about it."

A gust from the Charles River passes through the pane. In a flash, you're draping the blanket across my shoulders.

"Thanks, but I don't need this," I say, trying not to notice your warmth on the blanket, or the care you're taking to cover me with it.

"Keep it. You're cold."

"Temple!" Mrs. Lovecraft calls from the kitchen, and now her feet are on the stairs, light as a cat. Mrs. Lovecraft is light-footed, but her daughter is silent.

You meet your mother before she reaches the landing. "I heard Vivi coughing. I thought she might need a blanket. You told me to give her anything she needs." This leaves your mother with no response and you know this.

"Of course," your mother says shrilly. She turns to me. "You're not coming down with something, are you?"

Your navy eyes dance. We are in this together and this is what you wanted. "I'm not sick. I was—cold," I say.

Mrs. Lovecraft feels my forehead. "Henry keeps the thermostat at sixty-seven. We're used to it, I suppose. I'll speak with him. In the meantime, we've scheduled a physical for you tomorrow to make sure you're well."

My stomach drops. I don't need a doctor nosing around my parts, making comparisons between what was known about Vivi and what is visible on Jo. I open my mouth to say I'm not ready to have someone touch me, but Mrs. Lovecraft's small back is already winding down the stairs. Your eyes settle on me for a second, and inside my chest, I feel a tiny spark. You turn to leave.

"Thanks," I call. "For the blanket."

You stop.

Inside me, the spark throws heat.

"You're wrong, thinking I'm not happy that you're back," you say to the floor. "It's exactly what I wished for."

I squeeze a pillow against my chest hard and stare at the river. The sun drops, filling skyscraper windows and washing over the MIT dome. Then it falls into the river and sets it ablaze, then slips beneath the black water. The whole thing takes five minutes, maybe six.

A doctor's appointment could be the beginning of the

end. A missing mole, the wrong belly button, a comparison of ear shapes.

It's like Mrs. Lovecraft says: in this city, pretty doesn't last. But I think it will be worth every minute.

. . . . .

I have no idea what a doctor's office is supposed to look like. Momma was excellent at forging my school vaccinations, but mainly, I was healthy and lucky for it. When I got true-sick, like the time my appendix popped, Momma brought me to the emergency room at the hospital. This doctor's office is in Brookline in a building with a doorman and a marble-floored lobby stuffed with plants. Mrs. Lovecraft hits *B* for basement, and things change fast. In the hall, bare bulbs sizzle on the ceiling, and I can barely read the office numbers. It doesn't matter though, because the door we approach is unmarked. Mrs. Lovecraft looks over her shoulder before turning the knob, then dips her head into her chest and pushes me gently into the waiting room.

The rug is stained and the plastic orange chairs are empty. I sniff: mold and cigarette smoke. The receptionist desk is empty. I'm about to ask Mrs. Lovecraft if maybe the appointment is tomorrow when a man appears around the corner and introduces himself as Dr. Krebs.

He has long hands and his lab coat is dirty.

I follow Dr. Krebs into an exam room where the equipment looks hella old, and also, why the metal stirrups? I turn to ask Mrs. Lovecraft if this is Temple's doctor, but she's backed her way out of the room and shut the door. Dr. Krebs pats a cushioned table and I stare. He pats it again, and I realize he's telling me to sit, so I hoist myself up. He slaps a blood pressure cuff around my arm and sticks a thermometer in my mouth at the same time. When the cuff releases, he pulls out the thermometer and says, "Last period?"

"I don't get my period," I lie, because it's none of his business.

"Sexually active?" he says.

I look at him in horror. Where is Ginny when I need her?

"You know my story, right?"

He peers over his glasses at me. His eyes are rimmed pink and the lashes are sparse and that face has a lot of rodent going on.

"Are you sexually active?" he repeats.

"No," I say.

"Have you been sexually active?" he says.

"Shouldn't Mrs. Lovecraft be in here?" I say. I do not like this man, and I don't especially want Mrs. Lovecraft in here, but I'd also like these questions to stop.

"I'll give Mrs. Lovecraft my thoughts following the exam." He hands me a paper smock and tells me to undress except for my bra, which I should leave unhooked.

"What kind of an exam is this?" I ask.

"A thorough one. Look, Vivienne. The sooner you undress, the sooner you're on your way. We both have a job to do. Let's do our jobs."

My job is to be Vivi. Is his job to make sure? I wait for him to leave and yank my sweater over my head. He returns before I finish tying the smock. Holding up one long yellow hand, he says "No need," grabs my wrists and stretches my arms like wings, examining.

"Lie back, please."

Five seconds later, that yellow hand is in places I swore no man would ever go again. He keeps asking me to scoot down. I shut my eyes so tight they water. Finally, he's done.

"What was that for exactly?" I hiss, grabbing for my clothes. Vivi Weir might tolerate being groped, but Jolene Chastain freed herself from bad men, and she isn't having it.

He snaps off his rubber gloves and tosses them in the trash. "To determine if you're pregnant, and if you have any communicable diseases."

"Excuse me?"

"It's a routine exam, Vivienne. You can get dressed."

I get dressed, trembling to get in character, because Vivi couldn't have stood Dr. Krebs's grabby hands the way Jolene did—Jolene, who's had worse and got stronger for it. When Mrs. Lovecraft walks in, I leap for her, wrap my arms around her neck monkey-style, and cry. She strokes the back of my head and shushes me.

Dr. Krebs turns away coldly.

Mrs. Lovecraft unwraps my arms and smooths her hair. "I think we've had enough for one day. I'll call you from home and we can discuss the results."

"Sounds just right." Dr. Krebs sheds his lab coat like he wants to shed us. He is acting like a TV doctor forced at gunpoint into fixing a criminal's wound, and I resent that, because he doesn't know jack about me, and I sure hope it isn't going to be like this with every doctor/person who doubts that I am who I say I am, because then it's only a matter of time before their suspicions infect the Lovecrafts.

You might be infected already.

Mrs. Lovecraft extends her hand. "Thank you, Dr. Krebs."

Dr. Krebs shakes it, then pumps my hand with a smirk. "Welcome back, Vivienne. I hope you enjoy your new home."

We slip into a car that Mrs. Lovecraft has called up on her phone. City driving makes her nervous, she explains, so she leaves her big SUV home, in case Slade should need it. Which makes little sense, since Slade is apparently nocturnal. I'm starting to realize Slade's purpose seems to be to guard the Lovecrafts when they are home, which I guess is reasonable if your house is the kind of place children get stolen from.

As soon as we're buckled in, she starts.

"Dr. Krebs is not our usual family doctor. He's a friend of a friend, but he came strongly recommended, and he's discreet. It's better to avoid the more public places people expect us to go. Until we get our proper footing, see?"

I don't answer, because my head is against the glass and Dr. Krebs's manual explorations have me bugging. In Immokalee, I could shake bad thoughts by replacing them with good ones. The antidote to bad men like Dr. Krebs is Wolf. Wolf in our tent and the tire covered by the crusty tablecloth printed with strawberries. You couldn't set things on it, if we'd had things, because of the hole in the middle. The tire-table sat between his bed and mine, and by bed I mean crushed cardboard boxes covered with blankets. Mine has—had, I have to think Wolf is using it by now—that old foam egg crate underneath, which Wolf found but insisted I use. Two beds were silly, because not a night went by when I didn't end up freezing and curled next to Wolf, nose pressed to his skin, making sure he knew how much I liked it, because Wolf is not a boy who likes his own skin. If Wolf could, he would take off his own skin and leave it on a bus seat. Climb right off that bus and walk away from it.

Mrs. Lovecraft gazes ahead in her dark sunglasses.

I clear my throat. "The doctor had cold hands," I say.

The corners of Mrs. Lovecraft's mouth curl. She lets go of a laugh, a loose, beautiful sound, not like any I've heard before. The relief is sweet and I am glad I chose to say something dopey, because dopey is right, dopey works with these people.

"What Dr. Krebs lacks in bedside manner he makes up for in discretion," she says, giggling.

That word: *discretion*. Twice now she's used it. It's not often I have to look a word up, but I will when we get home.

That is not, however, the question I want answered right now. "Can I ask you a question?"

"What is it?"

"Is Temple glad that I'm back?"

Mrs. Lovecraft's forehead falls. She reaches for my hand, and hers is cool but mine is hot with fear. Is this where she says it's not working out? That I'll have to go away?

"We couldn't be happier," she says, still smiling.

I may not know every word, but I am a close listener, and We is not She. Mrs. Lovecraft sees I'm upset. She twists to face me and pulls my hands to her chest.

"Oh, hey! Did I tell you we have something wonderful planned for tonight?"

We have something wonderful planned. Still, We. When will We narrow down to You?

"Vivi?" Mrs. Lovecraft waves her hand in front of my face. "We're going to the symphony!"

. . . . .

There is a lot to this symphonying. A man came to fix Mrs. Lovecraft's hair right at the kitchen counter, which was both gross and fascinating. When he saw mine, Mrs. Lovecraft murmured, "Whatever you can do," a reference to the baby bangs I cut a month ago using nail scissors and a cracked compact mirror. The answer was a few passes with an iron that made things worse. In the end, he used extra-strength goop to slick back the bangs, and bobby pins from his magic black bag to tack my hair into a "messy bun" at the back of my head. I like the feel of it when I move. I can see myself in the door of the wall oven, and pulling hair away from my face shows off stuff I've never noticed. Like, that the line from my ear to my chin is pretty, or that my blue eyes, while wrong, are also big and bright.

We are late because you have the responsibilities that make you you, which means precalculus homework, a makeup cello lesson, and a meeting with someone called an organizational specialist. Mr. Lovecraft shoves the sleeve of his tux up to check his watch for the third time. He is a man tuxes were made for, but I try not to notice his hotness because he is my dad now and that is wrong. I shimmy around, uncomfortable sitting on the counter stool in a white collared dress that I would not have picked, but that is clean and nice, and thank God I figured out how to get tights on because Vivi was definitely a tights-wearer. When you finally come downstairs, you take my breath away. My expectation of fancy symphony clothes involved satin; and maybe, fur, and this is what I imagined you'd be wearing, but you are schooling me and I like it. Your black sweater is super-tight, and you're wearing a full, silvery-gray, stiff skirt, which is the opposite of tight, so tight on top, fairy godmother on the bottom, and *bam*: you are perfection. Instantly you teach me that my ideas of elegant are baby-ish, and I have a lot to learn from you, and I will and this is good.

"Darling, you're perfect," Mrs. Lovecraft says, finger-tips floating to her neck.

Mr. Lovecraft rises from his stool. "And we're off!"

Mrs. Lovecraft swoops to you, clutching a glittery bag with one hand and kissing you lightly on the forehead while you text and ignore her. Watching that kiss pokes me, as do all mothery things that Momma's last boy-friend took away from me, and I cannot get out of my own way about this, and I should because your eyes are suddenly on me.

"You look nice," you toss out, like you just remembered I'm here. I spent my day in a paper smock and stirrups thinking about Wolf but mostly about you, while you were at school, back in with your friends and things, and I am less important than I was yesterday. You said I was what you'd wished for, but you don't act like it. You're more interested in your phone.

"Are you mad about something?" you say flatly.

"No," I stammer, uncurling my balled fists. "I mean, what?"

You look to your mother. "She looks mad. Not now, but before."

Mrs. Lovecraft's brows pitch downward for a second. Then she laughs nervously and ducks into the hall.

"Vivi, I bought you a coat," she calls out. "You'll need to rip the tags off."

You squeeze your eyes and cock your head, studying me. I don't want to be studied. I slide off the stool to follow Mrs. Lovecraft out the door. I don't need to wait for you; we're not attached at the hip. My loyalty's not to you, it's to your mother and father—my mother and father.

Christ.

As we reach Symphony Hall, I start to shiver. It's the dress's fault. I don't love wearing dresses, and even with the babyish tights, I'm cold. Spring in Boston is colder than it ever feels in Florida, and one winter on these god-forsaken streets was enough for me. The snow that came days before Christmas was exciting for five minutes, until

I realized snow can kill you when you live in a tent. But I don't live in a tent anymore, I live with these people, and we are seconds from warmth. I've got this.

You give me a strange smile across the seat. I smile back coolly.

We park in an underground lot that surfaces on Massachusetts Avenue and wait until a cop whistles, signaling that we can cross. I stay close to Mrs. Lovecraft's heels as we enter under a neon sign that reads POPS in shouty red bulbs. A million people jam into the fancy lobby, and is this how we keep a low profile? Walls are painted gold, and stairs wind up, carpeted with velvet. I am inside a massive jewel box, with columns and high arched doorways and whirling servers balancing champagne on trays. The Lovecrafts hand me a program that says this is a special night for Boston executives: Presidents at the Pops. Would Vivi have come to this? There are a few kids, in ties and froufrou dresses and patent leather shoes. As we mingle our way through the lobby, Mrs. Lovecraft comes close to my ear, saying Boston is more like a big town than a city. This is an explanation for the people who stop us every couple of steps to chat. I am introduced as the Lovecrafts' "miracle," and I feel you stiffen every time it's uttered. You do not like this kind of attention, wouldn't court it if you had a choice, and this is going to be a problem for us.

A woman with bright lemony hair and a chiffon pouf on one shoulder leans over me.

"I wouldn't believe it if I didn't see it!" the lady exclaims, the champagne glass in her hand doing dangerous circles.

"Lanie!" Mr. Lovecraft says, sliding between the pretty lady and me and kissing her cheek. "You girls remember your third-grade teacher, Mrs. Higgins?"

My schoolteachers in Immokalee had big butts and angry lines between their eyebrows and didn't hang out at schmaltzy events. This woman has white-tipped finger-nails and she smells good.

"Retired now." Mrs. Higgins points the glass at me. "But I've never stopped thinking about you."

Mrs. Lovecraft starts in about the importance of taking my "reentry" slowly, but Mrs. Higgins isn't listening. "You were a joy in class, Vivi. Always so inquisitive, so open!"

I smile, and the effect is of a rabid dog.

Mrs. Higgins taps a nail to her forehead. "It's coming back to me now! A star reader, you were!"

My cheeks burn.

"You had the funniest habit of twisting your hair when

you were thinking hard," Mrs. Higgins adds, narrowing her eyes.

"We should probably be heading in," Mr. Lovecraft says, looking around. "The lights just flickered."

Mrs. Higgins juts her hip and leans back. "I'll never forget how adorable your costume was for the wax museum project! Do you remember what you wore?"

I feel your hand slip into mine. "Do you, Vivi?" you say.

My mouth twitches. This is a trap.

"You looked like the biggest dork, in a turtleneck and glasses, pretending to be Steve Jobs!" you say suddenly, laughing and swinging my hand. And you are in Mrs. Higgins's face, talking about how some science lesson she taught in third grade was the basis for an obsession with physics that drew you to fencing and . . .

. . . and I'm not following. Because all I can think of is how you rescued me from closer examination. There is love in the Lovecrafts' eyes, for each other and for you, and I have the sense you just did something wonderful. These are pretty people who wear their kindness on their pretty sleeves, and these are my people. They are named correctly, they understand the craft of love, and I am further away from Tent City than I ever imagined. Mrs. Lovecraft pulls me closer and Mr. Lovecraft puts his arm around his wife and around you, and the four of us politely excuse ourselves from tipsy, dangerous Mrs. Higgins and make our way into the music hall.

I look up. My library is beautiful, but this place is beautiful-magical, a pop-up book of fairy tales, where Cinderella lost her shoe. It is made of cream cheese ribboned with gold. Crystal chandeliers drip from a honeycombed ceiling. Statues rise from shallow caves in the walls, and on the stage, empty white chairs and music stands crowd the floor. People fill every seat, even the three levels of balconies surrounding us, above.

You tug my hand. "Time to sit." You lead me down a long aisle to seats so close we can touch the stage. We settle in chairs around a small table. "You don't remember this place, do you?"

I pretend I can't hear you above the roar of people.

"Our families came to the Presidents at the Pops together every spring," you continue. "We sat in floor seats just like these every year."

I let you pour me fancy water from a green bottle.

"It was a long time ago," I say.

"A lifetime," you say.

You fill in my blanks and it throws me. I'm relieved when the musicians appear onstage to applause. The conductor walks out last in a tux. He has a big personality but a little body, and he makes me smile when he talks to the audience, because he seems kind. He shrugs and raises his baton, and I become rigid in my seat, waiting, and the music is loud, and it fills my entire body. This is not the radio or the TV or the old laptop at Tent City someone jerry-rigged and I close my eyes and let it fill me. I feel the Lovecrafts watching, but I don't care. They get pleasure from seeing me happy, and maybe Vivi liked music too, and if she didn't, a girl can change.

Singers march out and line up in back. The conductor explains that the theme of the night is show tunes, and this is special. They launch into a bunch of songs that everyone seems to know, and the music swells, the end of one song running into the other, and the audience is supposed to sing along, so we do. To help us cheat, the words are projected on the wall behind the singers, and this is cornbally, old-fashioned fun, a sing-along with five hundred of your closest friends, and I can do this. Mr. Lovecraft has a smooth, deep voice, and I like hearing it rise above everyone else's, and we sway together as we sing. You hold back. Everyone knows your voice is better, and you use about 20 percent of it, which is classy and sad at the same time. Or maybe you can't use your whole voice because of the nodules thing, who knows? My heart is softening, and this is good but also dangerous. To have fun is to let down your guard.

The music slows for the last song. A girl strides out, some musical star, a skinny thing, in a sleek purple gown, and she's our age—mine, Temple's, Vivi's—or close. She cradles the microphone like a pro, and I wonder if that's how you held your mic when you were on that talent show. The words on the wall disappear: it is no longer our turn to sing. Everyone hushes, and I find myself moving to the edge of my seat. When she hits the first note, it is pure and un-showy and the opposite of every song that came before.

On my own
Pretending he's beside me.

My breath catches in my chest. I do not want, do not need a song to make me feel.

All alone
I walk with him till morning.

Too soon. I've had a year to learn how to swallow the pain of Momma, but not nearly enough time to take losing Wolf. This song and these words are choking me.

Without him.
I feel his arms around me

Tears, hot and fresh, well up. I need this to stop RIGHT NOW.

And when I lose my way I close my eyes
And he has found me.

The sobs seize and rack my body. I gasp to stuff the cry back inside. I leap from my seat and run for the nearest exit, climbing over bare legs and tuxedo pants and stepping on purses and breaking the things inside. I don't know if I'm being followed and I don't care: I should not make a scene, don't want to make a scene, and I'm so out of control I can't think myself out of this. I fly into the ladies' room past an attendant with wide eyes and slam the stall door.

Resting my forehead against the metal wall, I push out a hard breath.

"Vivi?"

You. You followed me.

"Don't try to talk," you yell from behind the door. "I know this is hard. That song: 'Pretending he's beside me.' The words trigger you. You miss your dad, obviously." You pause. I imagine ladies in gowns passing in and out, and wonder if they are whispering *Lovecrafts* behind their hands.

"That's it, isn't it? You miss your dad?"

I brush my nose with my wrist, hard. *It's a gift, Jo. Take it.*

I raise the bathroom lock and crack the door. "I do. I miss him something awful."

"Would it help if I told you that performance—in fact, this whole place—kills me inside?"

I step out slowly, my puffy face reflected back in the mirror. You move to the mirror beside me. "What do you mean?" I say.

"That girl up there? That should be me. I had everything: an agent, a contract. But I busted my own voice and lost any chance I had."

I turn to face you, but still you stare in the mirror, as though you're talking to that girl, the prettier one without the snot and tears.

"My whole life, I've been able to make everything I want to happen," you say. "By talent."

Jo is a talented con.

"By luck."

Jo was lucky to meet up with Wolf.

"Or by force of will."

Jo forced herself inside Vivi.

"I get that," I say.

"Except for the one thing I want," you say.

Jo could not keep her momma alive. I swallow. "I get that, too."

"My body betrayed me. My throat is thick with scars. I'll never be able to force it to do what I want it to do again."

"You can't sing even one note?"

"Not in a way that's worth it."

"But if you really like to sing, isn't any way worth it?"

You smile sadly in the mirror. "If only it were that simple."

"I don't understand," I say, reaching for tissues to wipe my red nose.

You throw back your shoulders and puff your chest. "Anyway. It is what it is."

I don't believe you think *it is what it is* for a minute.

You lock arms with me, wordless now, and we walk back to the hall as sisters, me a little messier, you a little more relaxed, into the music and to our parents. The conductor is letting a man named Connolly conduct. The orchestra plays on while the guy obviously doesn't have a clue, and everybody thinks it's a hoot.

You laugh, lusty. "I never understand what difference it makes if the conductor waves his little baton or not."

I squeeze your arm a little tighter. "Neither do I."

. . . . .

I seem to be on lockdown.

Also: there is no discussion of school, or checking in with Ginny, or the cops, and will I ever get to be with you? I have never met anyone with so many places to go and things to do. I wish hard on spending time with you, and you seem to want to spend time with me, but day after day it doesn't happen. How are we supposed to be sisters if your mother keeps us from being together, and she has done this, for seven days now, with excuses ranging from homework to lessons to getting more sleep. I can't help thinking that it will happen every new day, that we will connect, you spreading your shine onto me, wanting to, even though my real self is in disguise. The intuit in me feels it.

On Friday when I hear you come in from school at the unusual hour of Actually After School, I nearly trip running down the stairs. Mrs. Lovecraft has her head in the refrigerator, asking about your homework.

"I have tons of precalc, and I can't work here. I need to go to the library," you say.

"I'll call you a car," Mrs. Lovecraft says, muffled.

"We'll take the train," you say.

Mrs. Lovecraft backs out of the fridge. "We?"

"Vivi and me. What, is she going to keep hanging around here day after day with you?"

I cringe. I can't go to the library because of the small matter of Brown Tooth knowing where I belong, and it's not with you. I might be clean, and in clean clothes, but I still look like me, if you knew me.

Mrs. Lovecraft flashes tight palms. "Hold on. I'm not sure about you two going alone—on the train alone—together."

My cheeks pink just thinking about it.

"You can't keep Vivi bubble-wrapped forever, Mother," you say with an edge that would have sent Momma looking for a belt.

Mrs. Lovecraft licks her lips and becomes very still. You cock your head and stare her down. Finally, Mrs. Lovecraft says, "Well, I suppose it can't hurt. Here, you'll need this." She tears through her purse and fumbles with her wallet zipper, digs out a twenty and hands it to me.

"What's this for?" I say, because libraries are free.

"You can't go out without money, silly," she says.

In a flash we are gone, you with a pack on your back and me tagging along in the hoodie you tossed me, clutching the insides of my pockets and my unnecessary twenty. You walk like you mean it, leaving the smell of clean hair in your wake. I hope that Vivi, after being held captive and abused, would walk like I already walk out of habit. Street people cave their chests and keep chins tucked, unless confronted, which is when they fill themselves with air and take up space. I don't get the sense that Vivi ever took up much space in her life, so I shape myself into my usual comma and drag along.

We stop at a light and I catch up. "Thanks for taking me," I say.

You pull one earbud out and stare.

"I said thanks for taking me along," I repeat.

"Of course." You fumble with the earbud and pop it back in. "I wasn't going to leave you alone with *her*."

You confuse me. Your mother is kind, and you ought to know how lucky you are to have *her* and this and you leave me off balance in a way that sets my chest on fire.

"I feel like a tagalong here. It's not as though I have homework."

I can't tell if you can hear me or not. I try again.

"I mean, I guess they'll be sending me to school again sometime soon. It's just, no one's talked about it yet, and it's, like, still the school year."

More walking.

I try one more time before we duck into the subway station. "We don't have to be best friends again."

You pluck both earbuds out and pause, your whole face rearranging in thought. It takes you almost a minute to return to me.

"That's where you're wrong," you say. "We absolutely have to be friends again."

. . . . .

Clean clothes and a sparkly companion aren't going to help me if Brown Tooth is working. And she's always working—unlike you, whose sunken backpack contains no precalculus book, something your mother didn't notice but I did, and when do you study, anyway, to keep up all that sparkle?

At the main entrance, the iron lanterns have spikes meant for stabbing things, and the wind on the library plaza beats us back. I pull the hoodie around me as we are swept inside with a rush of tourists taking pictures of the white marble plaques, and I want to warn them it's too much to take in, I've tried and it is dizzying, and you are gone. I look for you up the stairs; no tight back, no swinging hair. I look to the security guard, but he looks into his phone.

I look to the massive sculpted lions on the first landing, but they are bored. I imagined we would go to Bates Hall, the place where I first found you tucked into a carrel with your same old book. I still imagine this.

I climb the marble stairs.

"Vivi!" you call over the tinny roar. You are below, at the start of a hall that leads to the bathrooms. You wave and I fight against the crowd. When I reach you, you look confused.

"Where were you going?" you ask.

Vivi would not know this place, would not remember it. A nine-year-old girl does not go to the public library. Unless she did. Maybe you and Vivi came here as kids: you lived a short T-stop away.

"I just figured we'd go where everyone else was going," I say brightly.

"But not where I was going," you say.

"No," I say cautiously.

The corners of your lips turn up, a hint of mocking. "Then you have changed."

You spin abruptly and I follow you down a hall where the gold fades. Thankfully, this is not Brown Tooth's beat, this is no one's beat, and the hall is empty. After several turns we arrive at a bronze elevator.

"I want to show you something," you say, hitting the up button.

The ancient elevator is slow to come, and our broken reflections shimmer back at us. When it does arrive it is confusing, with a button labeled STACK SIDE and other buttons, and I can hear pistons and gaskets as it moves, and this steampunk-y elevator is why I love my library, but I try not to let love relax me. You punch Three with the side of your fist and hold the rail. The ride is slow and jerky and I feel sick, but maybe that's fear. We exit the elevator and my legs wobble.

A sign says RARE BOOKS LOBBY AND SPECIAL COLLECTIONS, with an arrow.

"This is where you go to work on precalculus?" I ask.

"Something like that," you say, smiling.

We stop at a window facing the empty courtyard below, a pretty place where people with money eat in warm weather. You exhale sharply, fixed on getting what you want to say right.

"I'm going to be honest. At first, I didn't know how I felt about getting you back."

"I figured."

"What I mean is, I have loads of friends, but I haven't had a friend like you since you've been gone."

The words *been gone* instead of, say, *were kidnapped* are weird, and I will chew on that later. Now my eyes travel across your face: the wide-set eyes made wider by the middle hair part, the chin that tips up, the lips with their excessive softness. Are you beautiful, or are you strange-looking? Why can't I decide? And what does *a friend like you* mean?

You register my silence. "Was that weird to say?"

Silence does work best with you! Now I am in control. "It's fine. Show me what you want to show me."

You sigh and curl your arm around mine, and we are back on the right track. It's like I'm slipping into your mission, whatever that is, and though my whole life has been spent getting ready to go on missions—the stings, the scams—I've never been glad about it. The inside of your arm is cool, and touching you is making parts of me flame, and this has happened before, feeling pleasure when I should be repulsed, or at least, feel nothing. You lead me to a room called ART, a topsy-turvy room with long, empty tables and statues of nude Greeks and one clock that reads 10:58 over another clock that reads 8:53. Out of habit, I look for the adult: a librarian focuses hard on shuffling papers at her desk. Before she can register us, you pull me through this strange room to another, lined with iron balconies that lead to locked rooms with glass doors. The Koussevitzky Room is dim and medieval and the kind of place normally I would love to explore, but you drag me through another door. A sign tells me we are in the lobby for the RARE BOOKS AND MANUSCRIPTS DEPARTMENT, which sounds like a place Momma would have liked because rare means money. There is an adult here, too, but this librarian cares that we are here, because whatever is behind this door is worth something.

You drop my arm and at once I am cold.

The librarian shoves clear plastic glasses up her nose and smiles. She's not much older than us, but in my world, this is a bad thing, because the older they are, the easier they are to con, and I have to remind myself that the only person I'm conning is you. And you want to show me something, which I'm getting excited about, because this place is nerd heaven. Something awesome hits me: maybe Vivi was smart, book smart, or else she wouldn't have been friends with you, and this means I get to be book smart, too.

This is the role I was made for.

The young librarian holds the school ID that you passed her, but it's not the red Parkman School ID that I stole. It is blue and white and says Lasell College, and the little face in the square is not Temple Lovecraft, though it's close. The young librarian blinks behind her glasses and says it's nice to see you again, but she doesn't mean it, because she is bored with her job, and though this room is loaded with ancient books tied with string behind glass, it has to be hard, without daylight, and with the hum of wandering tourists who see books as objects and not ways to learn things. You slide out a superlight, superexpensive laptop and hand the librarian your backpack, too.

(I can't help it. This is how I see things. Expensive, not expensive. Worth stealing, not worth stealing.)

Now you're filling out a card to explain our purpose for going into the next room, and I want to know what that purpose is, but you're done and the librarian is buzzing us into the next room, blue with artificial light. The light is awful but the smell is not: I breathe deeply. It is the smell of ancient things. Shouty signs read STAFF ONLY BEYOND THIS POINT and THIS AREA IS UNDER VIDEO SURVEILLANCE.

"Be very specific today ladies," calls a woman beelining toward us, a Mad Hatter type, oddball, speedy. She is tall with a white buzz cut and is slightly scary but you are not scared. You smile and thank her and promise to be specific in your searches, as always. My eyes go to the other three people in the room, each at a different table, the way New Englanders sit. They each have one file folder and a laptop, except for an old man who writes by hand. One, a dreadlocked girl, is taking pictures. They are all lost in their work, and that looks nice to me; peaceful. You place your computer at the only empty table and walk away from it, a casualness only rich people have with expensive things, toward one of the big bureaus filled with drawers and topped with jars of scrap paper and stubby pencils. I am about to find out what "very specific" means. You pull open a drawer labeled DI—DY, filled with cards. It's nicely old-fashioned. You scribble something onto a slip of paper, do the same at a second drawer, and return both slips to the lady, who disappears into the back room. A man comes out to take her place, and because I am a student of people patterns, I get it: we're not allowed to be alone in this room. No one is. This room is full of valuable things, and I wonder how one would get away with stealing them, and something new hits me—shame—because these are not thoughts Vivi would have.

"What did you request?" I ask; a nice, normal question.

"The Poe and the Dickinson. For our project," you say, the last part overloud, though the man who replaced the lady is not listening. I must seem dense to you, but that is fine, because Vivi's brain would not go directly to *cheat* or even *steal* like mine does. We sit in the hum of the humidifier and quiet taps on keyboards and whooshes of a phone camera. The old man falls asleep on his arm and begins to snore. None are the sounds that I know and love: the hushed tones, the squish of wet boots, the phlegmy coughs you hear in this cold city.

When the replacement librarian takes a call at his desk, I whisper, "Why are we here?"

"Because this is where the good stuff is," you whisper back.

The lady hurries out with three long folders. She warns us to keep them flat and not to use a flash if we take pictures. We lean and almost touch heads. Your clean smell is yum and I am looking at Poe's "The Raven." Poe's handwriting is impossibly neat, almost girly. Nothing's crossed out, so either the dude was on his game or this is a later copy. At the bottom, it says *Edgar A. Poe*; swirly, a ta-da at the end. It's cool, and I have the sense I am looking at something I shouldn't.

"What's it about?" I whisper.

"Basically, a guy misses his girlfriend, gets crazier and crazier, and by the end he realizes she's dead and he's never going to see her again," you explain.

"And he needs a bird to tell him that?"

"Apparently."

We laugh at the same time. *Apparently.* I like the way you talk. I would like to sound more like you. I ought to sound more like you. The lady, who has now replaced the man, gives us a sharp look, and I like being bad with you. You slip the poem back into its folder and pull out a letter dated February 14, 1849, that's addressed to F. W. Thomas.

"This one's awesome," you tell me. "He's trashing Bostonians. Check it out."

Bostonians are really, as a race, far inferior in point of anything beyond mere talent . . . decidedly the most servile imitators of the English it is possible to conceive. It would be the easiest thing in the world to use them up en masse. One really well-written satire would accomplish the business. But it must not be such a dish of skimmed-milk-and-water as Lowell's.

"Satire?" I say.

"Yup. He's saying they are fools and easy to fool. And he wants to skewer them, not be wimpy about it like the other author, Lowell." You pull your hair back in an elastic, popping your ribs, enjoying the stretch. I feel the stretch in my own spine and arch my back.

You catch me mirroring you. You like it.

Before I can make a joke, you hide your smile behind your hand and point to the gray paper. "See here? What's cool is that you see this brilliant work. Then you see the man, who's kind of a snob. The two are not the same. Here, in this strange, sterile little place, you find the truth. Poe's work doesn't define him." You press your lips, staring at the page.

I might speak rougher than you, have a rougher mind than you. But it doesn't take Einstein to tell me that you're saying your work as a first-rate student doesn't define you. You can relate to Poe, and that's how it is with rich girls who have everything. You're always looking for someone to relate to you. If you knew who I really was, maybe you'd be saying my work as a con doesn't define me, either. I like this unfolding of you, ribs popping, knobby parts revealed. The air here is dead and switched on at the same time, and I wonder how often you come here for answers, and if there are answers here that will define us. Definitions would be good: you are Temple, and I am Vivi, but are we friends?

We say nothing for a while, staring at Poe's snobby letter. It is cold in this room and the librarians change shifts. Your eyes flick up when they pass. My stomach growls. I haven't eaten since breakfast, and it's funny how Mrs. Love-craft can be so careful about some things and so forgetful about others. I am on the verge of asking about "the Dick-inson" you'd asked to see along with "the Poe" when the sleeping man releases a death rattle.

You rise. "Time to go," you say, tucking your laptop under your arm, heading through the door and into the dark lobby, past the desk where we were buzzed in.

"What about your bag?" I call helpfully.

You stop short and turn, smiling tightly. The librarian hands you your backpack and computer case and once again you are off.

I scramble to follow.

"Where are we going?" I ask stupidly. This is becoming my thing, asking Nervous Nelly questions: straight man to your zany. Maybe it was Vivi's thing, too.

"To have fun," you reply.

Fun is not the word I would choose to describe librar-ies. I'd go for *safe, clean,* even *warm.*

"I'm in!" I say.

"That sounds like the old Vivi," you say as the door closes behind us in the Koussevitzky Room. "Do you know that you can't be videotaped in a public building if there isn't a sign warning you that you're on camera?"

Um, yes. "I did not know that."

The room has huge posters that show Koussevitzky was a conductor, and the room is encircled by a rickety-looking inner balcony. I'm wondering if we're going to scale the balcony, but you're already at the door to another room with a sign that says DWIGGINS.

"Be prepared for your mind to be blown," you warn. You are cute and devilish and you think this is so crazy, and I'm starting to get you, Temple Lovecraft. This is your way of rebelling, pretending to be a college student to look at musty pieces of paper and breaking into secret rooms without permission, and you're adorkable.

You slip inside and I follow. We're surrounded by lit windows. Behind the glass are wooden puppets on strings. There's a tin man, a bearded magician, and a beanie-wearing dude with a long black cigarette and a rabbit. There's a dragon. A floating ghost-skeleton and a juggler. This is the stuff of nightmares and this is what you get off on and you are a freak. Above each scene is another lit window, where the puppet handles are, crosses of wood with strings, and they look unattached.

"Cool," I whisper, because this seems like a place where you whisper. But really, I don't want to wake up those puppets. "It's like they're not even on strings."

"It's an illusion. If you did cut their strings, they'd collapse," you say.

You have a soft spot for these puppets, and I'm a sucker for soft. I cannot imagine having affection for anything so creepy, and it puts me in mind of Keloid Kurt, a scarred dude in Tent City who kept a mangy pet rat that he would stroke and coo at. Because I am smart, I see you are trying to tell me you feel like a puppet with that pressure to be perfect, with your parents controlling the strings, and I am moved.

"They're really cool, Temple. Thanks for showing them to me."

"Do you want to see how they're made?"

You also like to teach, and I am guessing Vivi liked to be taught. Living in someone else's skin is a lot easier when I'm being led.

"Yeah, totally."

We leave the room of the wooden undead, and there are official-looking visitors who probably know the room is off-limits, so we have to hang and pretend we had special permission to be in there. You drop to the floor, crisscross applesauce, and ask me to dictate notes to you about the puppets, and I'm left making things up like, "The floating ghost-skeleton is approximately twelve inches in height and represents man's inhumanity to man," as the visitors look on, impressed. I am pulling this out of my butt, something I read in a book once, and they nod and smile. You hang your face over your keyboard and try not to laugh. The visitors lose interest and leave.

"Impressive. You don't sound like someone who missed years of school stuck in a shed," you say, throwing your laptop into its bag and zipping it fast, but before I can stress about my carelessness you grab my elbow and drag me into the next dark room, laughing, fumbling for the switch. When the lights go up, we are in Frankenstein's laboratory. Headless wooden bodies lie in lines on a worktable. One has holes at the tops of its thighs, and we peek inside. There are sharp tools, crude mechanical tools, and something that looks like a vise. This is where the magic happens. Men should not play with dolls, and although you're supposed to think *tinker*, I am thinking *torture*, and I have no need to be in this room longer than necessary.

"They're harder to control than they look," you say. I wonder how much time you have spent playing with puppets, but it makes sense, since you've got the kind of rich family that would be big on expensive, "classic" toys.

"I bet." It sounds stupid and way overboard and you look at me and burst out laughing.

"Not that I've spent much time playing with puppets," you say.

"Not that I've spent that much time playing," I add, and it's okay to say that, because even if it's because I've been working cons my whole life, it could also be because I spent half my life in a shed.

You just think I'm being funny.

"Not that I would play with freaky wooden puppets if I could," you say.

"Not that those freaky wooden puppets wouldn't spring to life and attack you if you did," I say.

"Not that that's not exactly what happened to this Dwiggins dude," you say.

"Not that that's not exactly the way the Dwiggins dude wanted it to go down," I say.

"We're not being respectful."

"You're right. Rest in peace, puppet master. May you always feel a cool wooden hand on your back . . ."

"And the tug of a string at your shoulder."

"Nice! Amen."

"Amen." Your eyes go flat. "When did you get so funny, Vivi Weir?"

My throat catches. "I've had some time to work on my material."

You hold your stomach and wag your finger at me. "Very nice!" You check your watch. "We better go. After you."

We are becoming easy in each other's spaces, and this is special. You shut off the light and the door slams behind us. We laugh as we make our way back through the near-empty halls and it gets louder as we get closer to the bigger rooms where the unspecial people flock to so they can check stuff off their unspecial, touristy lists.

We huddle together as we head for the Copley Square train stop, and it is early for friendly huddling, but what the heck, I go for it. Though you are tall and Y-shaped where I am small and on the scrappy side, we fit nicely together, and you smell less like clean and more like candy. You pass me a stick of black licorice. Black licorice reminds me of the NyQuil one of Momma's boyfriends sipped when he had the shakes, but I've never tried it, and if there was ever a time to try new things, it's now. I chew, thinking how the library was my old safe place, a habit. I don't need it as my safe place anymore, and it's time for new habits, like eating black licorice. You duck down the subway stairs. I turn to look at the library, the stick of licorice flopping from my mouth, when I hear it.

"Jo!"

I freeze. My mouth falls open. The licorice drops.

Wolf rises. He was sitting on the library steps as I walked down. I must have strolled right past him. And now I know that I did; he was the boy my eyes saw but my mind didn't, with his face hidden in his knees and his sneaker tapping. Now I see his eyes are shaded gray and he is in a bad way, on or off something.

A wave of guilt and sickness washes over me. My mouth moves, but nothing comes out.

"Vivi!" you yell, commuters swirling around your up-turned face. "We're going to miss our train!"

Wolf's jacket flaps in the wind and he extends his hand toward me. His wrist is pale and thin. I feel your eyes on my back, impatient. Wolf is sinking and reaching for me and I have to go.

"I'm so sorry," I mouth to Wolf.

His eyes storm. Wolf is a boy who becomes more beautiful when he rages, which is why he glazes over when he hustles. People walking past eye him, and though he is obviously homeless, his beauty is magnetic, and those who can't have him will stare. A middle-aged man in a suit stops and says something to him. Wolf stares only at me. He tells the man something—his fee, I know this—still looking at me. I know this is one of those moments that I will regret the rest of my life, but yours is not a life I can live, and Wolf, I need to leave you.

"I have to go." My whisper is lost in the length between us.

"Vivienne!" you call over the screech of the inbound train. You're fidgeting halfway down the stairs, looking at the train over your shoulder and back at me.

You throw up your hands, mouthing, "What the?"

When I turn back around Wolf is in front of me.

I have exactly one choice. I dig in my pocket and pull out the twenty-dollar bill. I hand it to him, and say loudly, "God bless."

I run down the stairs, pressing my fist into my mouth to hold back the sob.

· · · · ·

We're getting knocked around, holding the same train pole when you ask me why I gave that street kid money.

"I felt sorry for him. Pay it forward, you know? Make the world a better place," I say, looking at a spot on the floor.

"That's a generous outlook for someone who's been through what you have," you say.

I'm grateful when the train stops and a mob of people press in. I make a big deal out of rearranging myself, pretending to forget your question. But you stand with your feet planted, hardly noticing people cramming around you, some fixing dirty looks.

"I mean, I'd be hating the world right about now," you say.

"I try not to focus too much on what happened," I say, squirming.

"In the shed?"

"Yes." I stare hard at the top of a child's head.

"We all have pasts we can't change. Would you rather not talk?" you offer.

I nod. You smile and shift to give me room. The rest of the ride we're silent and this is a good thing, because I can hardly hold myself together after having seen Wolf, and you think I'm having Bad Shed Thoughts. I imagine Wolf waiting for me to come home the night that I left, then the next morning, and the mornings after that, choosing not to believe I won't come back. His saying nothing as I passed him on the library stairs was strange and unexpected and I am grateful. The pain isn't the same as when Momma died. It's loss dunked in guilt, and I hate myself so much I want to bite my fist. As we walk down Commonwealth Avenue and approach the brownstone, I shove my hand in my pocket to keep from biting it. My fingers brush something velvety. I stop and pull it out of my pocket. You sense I'm not behind and turn at the top of the stairs. Your hair, loose now, lashes your cheeks in the wind.

You wear a small smile.

I blink in disbelief at the scrap of paper between my fingers. The year 1866 is scribbled with faded pen strokes, and the words PROPERTY OF BOSTON PUBLIC LIBRARY are stamped inside a red oval.

"It's fine," you say, climbing down slowly. When you reach the last step you giggle, brushing a loose hair from my cheek. "I won't tell my parents you stole it."

· · · · ·

A death blow
is a life blow
to some
Who till they
died did not
alive become.
Who had they

lived, had died
but when
they died,
Vitality begun.

I do not appreciate having this and this is wrong and you know it. There is no way to return it and we are on camera and it's on record that we were the last ones to have it. Now I'm stuck waiting until you get home to explain how we're going to fix this. You hid from me all night and I heard you leave in an Uber early this morning, while I was still in bed, and you have my precious parts in your hand right now.

And yet it is cool, owning something that was written by a famous poet in 1866. I wonder what the value of an original Dickinson poem is. The Lovecrafts haven't given me access to the Internet, not that I'm stupid enough to do searches anyway. I mostly care about this because it's going to piss the Lovecrafts off. They can never know. You are sneaky and a troublemaker, but you are also warm and goofy, and this is your idea of fun.

I brush my teeth like mad, because Vivi's teeth were bright and strong.

"Vivi?"

I spray the mirror with Crest. Mrs. Lovecraft stands

behind me. I cringe, dabbing at the mirror with a towel too fancy to be used to clean up toothpaste, and then cringe at that, apologizing.

Mrs. Lovecraft reacts to none of it. "I wondered if we might have a word?"

This is it. I am going down. Temple, you are a foxy trickster, and this is your way of getting rid of your unasked for, unplanned for new sister, the reappearing playmate you didn't want or need, given your "loads of friends." I was a fool to think this would work.

"Sure. Should I get dressed?" I ask, pointing at my pajamas, which probably cost what Wolf earns in an hour.

Wolf.

"Just come down. We'll talk over breakfast."

I stop in my bedroom and shimmy into my bra underneath my pajama shirt. My MO is zero sexuality in the Lovecraft household, not only to remind them of forever-nine Vivi, but also to avoid threatening my new mother, because, been there. I pad down the stairs, still feeling naked in my pajamas, the polished steps slippery under my socked feet. In the kitchen, Mr. Lovecraft stands with his back to me and his phone held to his ear with one broad shoulder, and Mrs. Lovecraft is seated at the counter. A fourth stool appeared at some point and I have a spot, and at my spot sit fresh fruit and four kinds of granola and Greek yogurt and I will never get used to choices, though I would like to. Mrs. Lovecraft insists we can eat and talk at the same time, in fact, maybe she'll have some yogurt, too. (She won't. I haven't seen her eat a full meal yet.) I fill my bowl with yogurt and granola and fruit. As Mr. Lovecraft turns and catches sight of me, his eyebrows rise, because he has not yet watched me eat, though Mrs. Lovecraft is already used to my rough ways. Mrs. Lovecraft shoots him a look, and he ends his call.

"Where's Temple?" I ask between slurps and crunches. If they're going to toss me for stealing a valuable poem, I'm going to inhale as many calories as I can during my best last meal.

"It's Saturday. She has cello." Mrs. Lovecraft says this like the world knows Temple Lovecraft has a cello lesson on Saturdays. "Which works out well, because this is a conversation meant for us three."

Natch. Why involve your perfect daughter in the sleazy details of my crime?

"Okay," I mumble, wiping my mouth with my napkin. Mrs. Lovecraft looks to Mr. Lovecraft, who has shaved his beard as predicted. In sweatpants and a tee, he is more boyishly handsome than I thought, and she thinks this, too, the way she gazes at him, which is not the way he gazes at her. I make a mental note of this, because it could be useful in the future. Mr. Lovecraft sits awkwardly at the counter. His knees and elbows jut at strange angles, like yours. He is a man used to taking up space.

"As you can imagine, the police are very interested in catching your abductor. In fact, they won't let the matter rest until he is found," he says.

"They're doing their job, of course," she adds.

"But we understand your need to put this behind you. Not to allow this criminal to steal one more second of your precious life."

"Moving forward is best."

"Best for you. And what's best for you is our concern. Especially since you remember so little of your time in the shed, isn't that right?" he says, but maybe insists.

I nearly miss my cue, still thinking about Emily Dickinson in my underwear drawer filled by Mrs. Lovecraft with clean cotton wonderfulness. "Mmm."

"We understand that there is a perpetrator at large and that he could strike again. But here's the thing. If you remember so little—"

I never said that I remember so little. The second rule of conning: never forget what you claim.

"—then the chances of catching him are slim. Yet the police won't rest until they find him. There will be endless procedural interviews. They won't let you move on. But you have a choice here. You can make it stop."

"I can?" I say.

"You can simply tell the police that you made the story up. The truth is, you have amnesia. You have no idea where you've been these last seven years."

The Lovecrafts are freaking brilliant, smarter than me, smarter than Momma, smarter than you, Temple, thinking you got me into enough trouble that your parents would make me leave when they want me to stay.

But—Vivi is an innocent. Lying doesn't fly with Vivi. I screw my face into confusion and say, "You want me to lie?"

Mrs. Lovecraft shakes her head. "Not lie exactly. Just confess your uncertainty. Make it clear that you don't remember the details."

"You won't be alone. We'll be there, of course, and our attorney will be, too. His name is Gene. The goal is to make this one meeting; one and done. Any question you feel like you can't answer, don't worry. Gene will handle it."

"Gene is an old family friend, and he was a friend of your

parents," Mrs. Lovecraft says, licking her lips. "If you don't tell the police this, they will be a permanent fixture in your life. Relentless. If they find your abductor, there will be a trial. You will be questioned, ripped to shreds on the stand. Painful memories will be lived over and over. It takes away from the joy of your recovery."

I could not agree more.

"I really don't remember," I say softly.

Mrs. Lovecraft presses her fingers to her smile, and Mr. Lovecraft opens his palms. I am about to get a group hug. Mrs. Lovecraft rises and pulls me out of my seat to hug me and Mr. Lovecraft stands behind her with his hands on her shoulders, squeezing them, and I have yogurt on my shirt and it's getting on Mrs. Lovecraft's blouse and she doesn't see.

And like that Mr. Lovecraft is off to his fancy-sounding Equinox in the Financial District and you are tucked away at your fancy cello lesson and Mrs. Lovecraft and I are on fancy Newbury Street getting me a fancy haircut. Four fancies is okay here, because wishing is not needed. The hairdresser is respectful and gentle to the point of cringy. He speaks only to Mrs. Lovecraft, and they are close. Jerel has a studded belt and a goatee and is the same dude who came to our house before the symphony. He owns the place and speaks in soothing tones, as though his salon is a museum, and usually I don't like my head touched, but I wish the girl who washed my hair took even longer because who knew you could have your head massaged, and that it would feel so amazing? We are in a private room, which is the perk of being a Lovecraft. Mrs. Lovecraft perches on a white chair that looks like an alien pod and flips through a magazine.

I wait for the hairdresser to sweep away, murmuring about tinfoil, before I ask her the question I've been wondering.

"Will I go to school with Temple?" I ask. There are considerations to make, a hide to be grown. If they send me to your all-girls school, there's going to be a whole other level of questions and challenges. Also, math might not be my strong suit, but three years of no school do not equal seven years of no school, so I'm going to have to downscale my knowledge, do a little research on third-grade curriculum versus high school. I need to know what I don't know.

Mrs. Lovecraft repeats the question back to me. Then: "Oh no, that would never work! We've hired a tutor to homeschool you."

I exhale hard under my black cape. Jerel returns with

an assistant pushing a cart carrying a bowl of paste and tin-foil strips. I give the bowl a strange look, and he strokes my hair.

"We're going to brighten you up a touch," he coos. "Give you that sun-kissed look."

I've done everything to escape being sun-kissed. Florida was my purgatory and gray Boston is my salvation. Now they want me to look like I spend time in the sun, and that one photo I saw of Vivienne Weir is the reason. My hand floats to touch the foil strips that Jerel has painted sections of my hair to. I look like I'm trying to block aliens from reading my thoughts. Once, Wolf and I caught lice, and even though I haven't itched for months, I wonder if Jerel can tell. Lice look less like bugs and more like white glue, and they will live through the apocalypse. We slopped may-onnaise on each other's heads and wrapped them in Saran Wrap, and combed each other out like monkeys. The mayo took weeks to get rid of, and it occurs to me, gazing into depths of mirrors, that my looks are not nearly as fine as Vivi's. When I think I can't take it anymore, Jerel re-leases me from my tinfoil cage. Again, I am washed, and this is becoming my favorite part, and is this salon where Temple goes to get polished and rich-looking? Jerel raises his scissors and starts lopping hair off, big lengths of it, and it sails to the floor. No one asks me what style I want but I am silent, because this isn't about me, though I am in the chair. In fact, I am turned away from the mirror, facing Mrs. Lovecraft, who looks excited.

When Jerel spins my chair back around, I squeak.

The girl in the mirror is not just sun-kissed. She is waxed and buffed and downright sparkly. My hair is lighter. My hair is glossy. The baby bangs are blended and the ends turn under and it is shorter in a way that Wolf would hate, but I know this shorter is chic. I feel the back of my neck and it is cool and I do not recognize myself.

Mrs. Lovecraft leaps from her pod and clasps her hands. "So smart, Jerel! It's perfection!" She moves behind my chair and Jerel steps aside. In the mirror, her eyes shimmer with tears. "Vivienne Weir, you grew up to be a beautiful young lady."

After I unsnap the robe and Mrs. Lovecraft hands over her credit card, it is time to shop. You will not tolerate me wearing your old clothes forever, and Mrs. Lovecraft wisely bought me only underwear, pajamas, and one fancy coat, given the uncertainty of the situation. The jeans I'm wearing bite my waist and drag on the ground, and Mrs. Lovecraft seems to think an overcorrection is in order. We head for J.Crew to buy cropped pants and striped sweaters. Unlike at the salon, here she asks my opinion on what I like, and though I don't like anything here in this store of little-kid colors, I do like new things, and I like covering my body, and I like adding up the price tags in my head, which is dizzying. And I'm starting to understand why people equate stuff with love, because having your own nice clean things means you blend in without trying, and blending in is relaxing. By the time we've hit H&M "for some trendy things," we are laughing like mother and daughter, like ladies who lunch, and we do lunch, at Stephanie's on Newbury, where the hostess knows Clarissa Lovecraft and the servers fall over themselves to satisfy her, and by association, me. She gets me to try tuna sashimi, which is served in a cocktail glass with Day-Glo orange sprinkles. When I make a face, she swears I liked it as a child, and I can do this, I can eat this red slime so much like an internal organ, along with its tangerine sprinkles, and I do, and it is surprisingly good.

Mrs. Lovecraft orders a second cocktail, muttering "Uber," like I care if she drives drunk, me whose real mother lived high. She wishes out loud that we didn't have to carry so many bags. I like the bags, I tell her: there is something cool and old-fashioned about two ladies swinging overflowing shopping bags and smiling. She loves this and toasts my iced tea. There's only one thing that would make this better, she says. Would I mind changing into one of my new outfits? I skip to the ladies' room, ripping tags off a lime-green button-down sweater with an attached collar and cotton pants sprayed with teeny dots. I fold the clothes I was wearing and place them in the bag, then check myself in the mirror.

I expect to look dorky. I don't expect to look young.

Momma called me an old soul. Maybe the first half of my life, in Immokalee and the other blur-towns, was my time to be old. This is my time to be young.

I toss my hair around my face and practically skip back to the table, where a waitress is serving Mrs. Lovecraft her third vodka cocktail.

"Look at you! Camera ready, I'd say," she says, her words a little slurry.

I pull my seat in primly. "We're taking pictures?"

"You never know when the press are around, darling," she says.

. . . . .

I lay the clothes out on my bed. I'm trying hard to imagine the girl on the bus, how she would have acted if she saw me in one of these outfits. Her admiring looks, how we might have talked about her family in Boston, or she might have shown me what was in her suitcase. Instead, I see not empty clothes, but skinny, sprawled girls with busted limbs.

You knock and I jump. It is nearly nine p.m., and you're just getting home from a day that started with cello, moved on to back-to-back tutoring sessions, tennis, and finally, fencing. Yet you glow. You thrive on these overscheduled days, I am learning, and you did not spend the afternoon thinking about what you planted in my pocket.

You glance drily at the clothes. "Well, at least now you have the preapproved uniform."

"Why did you do it?" I ask.

"And the hair is a lot better."

I'm not biting. "The poem, Temple. Why did you steal it?"

You scan me, looking for anger you can react to, but I cleansed my words of it. I am better at this game than you, and it's time I proved it.

"Consider the poem my 'Welcome home, Vivi' gift," she says. "You don't like it?"

"We have to give it back."

"You can't give it back. But it doesn't matter. They can never track you down. We used a fake ID, remember?"

"You used a fake ID."

Your lip curls. "Fine, I used a fake ID."

"We can never go back to the library again."

"So we don't." You flop down on the bed, crushing an eighty-dollar T-shirt that says something in French. "Who cares?"

I do care. I can't let myself miss Momma, or Wolf, but I can miss the long table with rows of green lampshades, and my old spot in front of the fireplace among the busts of Lucy Stone, Alice Stone Blackwell, and Thomas Gold Appleton. I can miss the gold seam in the floor that divides the tiles cracked in patterns that I memorized. I can miss the high arched windows or the colorful flags whipping in the wind outside them. I can miss the carved white roses in the corners of the ceiling.

It's fine. I am safer here. I am safer here. I am safer.

(make it so)

I move to my underwear drawer and take the poem out. The delicate paper is stained and charred at one edge, like Dickinson tried to burn it. I perch on the bed's edge and read. " 'A death blow is a life blow to some, who till they died did not alive become. Who had they lived, had died but when they died, Vitality begun.' "

You scoot closer. "You didn't say if you liked it."

Vivi is simple. Vivi admits to not understanding things. "I'm not sure I understand it," I say.

You take it gently from my fingers. "It's here in the first line. A death blow is a life blow to some."

I think of Momma and her broken face. I think of Cold John, who, when everyone hauled over to the Father Bill's shelter one night last winter, stayed in his tent and never woke up. I think of when someone stole Keloid Kurt's rat and stuck it with a stick and roasted it over the fire. I think of the dead things I've seen, mothers and men and rats, and I know what dead is. The only people who talk about dead like it's something pretty and fanciful are people who haven't seen it up close.

"Isn't dead dead?"

"Not always. For some people, it's their first big shot at living. At least that's what Dickinson is saying."

You may be smarter than me at most things, but this is a topic I know way better than you, and I can't help myself. "Blow. She says 'death blow.' That's death by violence. How do you recover from that?"

"She also says 'life blow.' A life born from violence."

I shake my head. "She's talking about people who become more famous after death. Maybe she was thinking that would be her story."

"It was the case for Poe," you say as you rise. "Anyway, I thought it would speak to you. Because, you know, everyone thought you were dead."

Despite myself, I am touched. You are generous, it's true. You give things that mean things. Even if they can get me in trouble. Maybe this is what Vivi loved about you. Maybe you pushed Vivi into living on the edge.

Still. I need to pretend stealing is scary, me who has seen and done way worse. Jaded at sixteen, playing the innocent. I can do this.

"Thank you," I say. "It was wrong to steal. But it's the thought behind it that counts, right?"

You look at the floor, cheeks slack. "Give it to me and I'll take it back."

"You said there's no way," I say in a rush. Now I feel bad.

"There's always a way."

"They know you. I mean, by sight, anyway." Careful, Jo. Don't start giving advice from experience. "What if they call you out?"

"Narrow escapes are kind of my thing," you say, flashing a wicked smile. "Maybe I'll even use a disguise."

Oh my God. I picture you in a black bob wig and big sunglasses. It's so cute when a regular girl tries to play the con.

You study the clothes on my bed for a moment, those girls with their flung body parts. "On the topic of costumes, what are you wearing to the police station tomorrow?"

"I don't know." My voice hitches in surprise. You know I'm going to the police station? "Does it matter what I wear?"

"It always matters." You nod at my chest. "Wear that sweater. Preppy and innocent. And Henry and Clarissa's plan is a good one: say you don't remember a thing. No one presses the shell-shocked or the traumatized. Take it from me." I'm mouthing "Henry and Clarissa?" at your back when you turn suddenly at the door. "Another thing." You rush to hug me, press of hot sternum. "I'm glad you're back. It makes everything better."

I watch the door. Maybe you'll return, but you don't. I hear your music crank and disappear (you popped on headphones; I know your ways), and it's just me and the flat girls, and I know how they feel. Plucking them off the bed, I drape their arms and legs on hangers inside my empty closet. From the middle of my bed with my legs crossed, I admire my open closet and the clothes inside that are mine. Eventually, I flick off the light and climb into my bed, which I'm starting to look forward to, and I drift fast. This house seems to want me to sleep in it, and though it's hours earlier than I've ever slept, I oblige, and the fall is delicious.

A metallic rattle jolts me awake.

My window faces a back alley. While the first-floor windows are barred, the third floor is considered too high for breaking and entering, but I wouldn't mind some bars. Far as I'm concerned, a ladder leading to your window might as well be a stamped invitation. I feel under my pillow for the steak knife I stole from the kitchen—weak blade, but it'll do—and crawl off the bed, ninja-style, sliding against the wall. The fire-escape creep won't expect a girl who knows the best place for stabbing is the neck or groin. *Jangle, shake-shake, jangle.* Louder now. I tested that fire escape when I moved in, one leg out the window. It held good. A shade darker on the floor in front of the window: the city light gives his shadow away. My back prickles.

He stands on the landing looking directly into my room.

I have two choices: scream or fight. Vivi would scream. Jo would fight.

I leap off the wall, knife blazing.

Wolf throws up his hands and lurches backward, veering wildly toward the rail.

I drop the knife and reach fast for a handful of his shirt, yanking him inside. He falls into me, and we stagger for a minute like we're dancing drunk until I shove him off.

The bedroom is dark but I can see the cut on his lower lip. He has a need in his eyes for something barbed or burning, a need he can fight when he has me.

"You look like someone else," he says.

"You look the same," I whisper. Over my shoulder, I check through the crack in my door to see if your light has flipped on. Still dark. When I turn, Wolf is circling the room. Even in the purple half-light, I can see that he is stunned by the grand curtains and poster bed and polished plank floors. I smell cold air and other men's skin, and I shouldn't care.

He could blow everything just by being here.

If we get caught I will accuse him of scaling the fire escape to rape me. He won't argue, because although he hates me right now, he also loves me.

Wolf makes a low whistle. "This is some place."

"You can't stay," I whisper, less sure than I ought to be.

"Don't plan to," he says, lifting a bell-shaped glass cover off a gold tree sitting on the dresser. "Unless they lost a boy here, too. Maybe I could play pretend-rich-kid alongside you."

"Wolf . . ."

"What is this thing, anyway?" he says, holding the glass cover in the air.

"It's a cloche. It holds jewelry. I mean, you hang jewelry on the tree and the glass covers it."

He widens his eyes, nodding. "Fancy. Cloche." He sets the glass bell down carefully.

"Why are you here?" I say, weighting my words.

He turns and looks me full in the face. "I could ask you the same question."

I move closer and force myself to breathe him in. The smell of the men on Wolf is enough to keep me away. I worked hard to keep Momma's men off me; it's a contamination and I am clean here in my new home and *backward* is not in my vocabulary. I do not want you, Wolf. I do not want you, Wolf. I do not want.

"I'm safe here. They believe I'm Vivienne Weir."

Something shifts inside him; he was waiting for this. "Safe from what?"

"The last one, for starters. What if he comes after me?"

"Your momma's been dead a year. No one's coming after you." He leans in and takes my chin. "That isn't why you left."

I step backward. "Maybe life in Tent City isn't for me."

"Because your life in Florida was so fine?" He waves his hands in the air. "Because this is what you're used to?"

"You wouldn't understand."

"Because I never had a mother? You aren't the only one who had a different life before Tent City."

"Fine. I couldn't take the life anymore."

"With me. You couldn't take the life with me anymore. Is that what you're saying, Jolene?"

I grab his wrists. The insides are marked by yellowed thumbprints. Wolf cannot protect himself from the things he lets happen to him because he thinks he isn't worth not letting things happen to him. I am scared for Wolf. I am scared for me. Mostly, though, I know life in Tent City isn't the life I'm supposed to have. Life in Immokalee with Momma wasn't, either. I've been inside other people's lives, and I found out what I was missing, and it looked a lot more like this.

"Listen to me. Being Vivienne Weir gives me a home. A real home, Wolf! And a life. Already, they want to keep me safe. I told them I was abducted and kept in a shed, but they've got me changing my story because they don't want the police bothering me about catching the perpetrator. They have private security because Mr. Lovecraft is a big deal in this city, he's built the whole skyline, and he's had threats, and they worry about their daughter, too, since the real Vivi disappeared from their own house, this house, seven years ago."

"It's only a matter of time before the police dissect your story and trip you up. It's too complicated. Keep the con simple. You told me that one yourself. You've already forgotten the rules of being Jolene Chastain."

"That's because I am Vivienne Weir." I say it in my head two more times, and Wolf is talking, but I can't hear him.

"You might be a good con. But you can't keep it up. Then your cover will be blown and they'll throw you back out on the street."

"I won't blow this."

"You think I'll be there when you wake up from your pretty dream, but maybe I won't be."

"There's no waking up from the return of Vivienne Weir! I am the living, breathing happy ending to a national tragedy. Jolene Chastain is dead. She has to be dead." I reach up on my toes and move hair from his eyes. "Please, Wolf. I need this."

Wolf pulls away and walks past the dresser, pauses, and I wince, waiting for him to smash the glass cloche. Instead he moves to the open closet and inspects the prim, pretty clothes and the clean shoes set on the floor beneath. He turns to face me, and I brace myself.

"What happens when this family figures out you're not Vivienne Weir?"

How do I explain the Lovecrafts to Wolf? The safety in Mr. Lovecraft's broad-shouldered disinterest when men have never been disinterested in me. Mrs. Lovecraft's warmth and ready closeness, her animal protectiveness of me, and of her daughter. The promise of Slade's easy violence. And then I think of you. Of the sense of being off-kilter and alive. You who gets me, who says it's better with me here. You who has the potential to be my first and only friend, a friend to fill the lonely space I didn't know existed until you filled it.

Who till they died did not alive become.

The idea of being ripped from the Lovecrafts is already too much to bear. Muscle ripped from tendon, the stripping of skin. This is my new fear: not Momma's murderer. I won't admit this, because I will hurt Wolf, and I am the only thing in this world that hasn't hurt him.

"Jolene."

"I don't know," I whisper, my voice catching on a sob.

Wolf cups the back of my neck and pulls me to his

chest. I breath in smoke, city, skin. My hunger for Wolf will fade; hunger always does.

"You'll need a plan if they find out," he says near my ear. "You'll need to disappear."

What Wolf doesn't know is that I've already disappeared.

"Promise me if you get in trouble, you'll send me a signal," he says.

I laugh sadly against him. "Sure. I'll beam my bat signal onto the night sky."

He pushes me away and rifles through his jeans pocket, finds a burner phone and presses it into my hand. "Take this."

I stare at the phone. "I can't have this. I don't own anything; everything is theirs. They'll find it." This is my second lie to Wolf. Truth is, I don't trust myself not to go back to him, and the phone is a temptation I can't risk.

"Hide it wherever you hide that knife you were ready to cut me with."

I grimace and shove the phone back at him.

"Fine. Tie that hideous sweater to the fire escape. That'll be our signal."

"Jolene Chastain doesn't needed rescuing."

"But Vivienne Weir might." He tosses the phone onto the bed and turns to go, stopping once to look over his shoulder, waiting for me to ask him to stay. The pain in his eyes is dizzying. I bite my lip hard until he leaves, climbing back through the window, shoulder blades jutting through his jacket. I breathe only after he leaves; as he came, on shaking metal scaffolding, hours closer to the pain he seeks.

In Tent City I had a dream that kept coming back, where Momma's last boyfriend and Wolf were sitting at a table set with china and flowers, and there was classic music, and Wolf was cutting off parts of himself and offering them to the Last One, and he was eating, and it was very civilized, and I would wake drenched in sweat with my heart beating inside my chest to be let out, grabbing under the blanket to feel Wolf's arms, hands, legs, ears, making sure the parts were attached.

Tonight, I wake twice from that same suffocating dream. Except this time, we are in the Lovecrafts' dining room, and I am with you, Temple, and we are eating as old-fashioned music plays, and I am afraid of what I am eating, but it is delicious, and I eat until I am full.

. . . . .

We are crammed in the detective's paneled office: Detective Curley behind the desk; Ginny, who has taken ownership of me since I entered the room, with an arm around the back of my chair; Mr. and Mrs. Lovecraft, him standing, her seated; and two men, the Lovecrafts' attorney, Lawyer Gene, and a stooped man named Harvey Silver, who knows Lawyer Gene and who seems to be on the same payroll, and by that I mean the Lovecrafts'. It turns out Harvey is a psychiatrist and a trauma specialist who has diagnosed me with dissociative amnesia along with repressed memory even though we met in the parking lot twelve minutes ago. Everyone is talking at once but me. It's a scene out of a black-and-white movie, when the bank is closing and everyone's about to lose their life savings.

Ginny slices the air with her hands and yells, "Hold up!" which is wrong for a fifty-year-old lady with too-long hair. Everyone stares at her in shock.

Harvey recovers first and sees his opening.

"Childhood trauma can result in difficulty with memory storage and retrieval. When a memory is forgotten, clinicians say that a likely explanation is dis-soci-ation." He says this like the detective is a little kid, and though Ginny nods nicely, I think Harvey is making the wrong play.

"Dissociation?" Lawyer Gene says. I cringe at the staged feel of it.

"Yes, Gene," Silver says. "*Dissociation* means that a memory is not actually lost, but is 'unavailable' "—air quotes; God—"for retrieval. That is, it's in 'memory storage' "—more air quotes, at which Curley rolls his eyes—"but cannot for a period of time actually be recalled."

"What's the bottom line, Mr. Silver?" growls Detective Curley.

"Doctor," Ginny corrects.

Everyone ignores Ginny, even Dr. Silver, who directs his answer to the detective, the only person in the room who needs convincing.

"It's Vivienne's way of protecting herself from the pain of that memory," Dr. Silver says.

When my name is spoken for the first time, everyone remembers I am there. They turn and look at me. I scowl.

"Dissociative amnesia has been positively linked to overwhelming stress caused by a traumatic event: an event suffered, or witnessed, or even simply imagined. Until those memories are unlocked, we will never know for sure."

"You're saying either she was abducted, or she saw someone abducted, or she imagined she was abducted? Fantastic," says Detective Curley.

"There isn't cause for sarcasm, Detective," says Mrs. Lovecraft.

"What my wife means, Detective, is that we understand your skepticism. It was hard for us to believe, too," says Mr. Lovecraft.

"Seven years is a long time to forget," Detective Curley says. "Can't she be treated to make her memory come back?"

I want to yell at this guy to take the excuse we're offering him and retire early. Boston must be a boring city if he's looking for stuff to do. A working vacation in Immokalee would keep his reflexes sharp.

"There are no laboratory tests to diagnose dissociative disorders. A doctor might use blood tests or imaging to make sure Vivi doesn't have a physical illness or side effects from a medication. She might be referred to a mental health professional such as a psychiatrist, psychologist, or psychiatric social worker who is specially trained to diagnose and treat mental illnesses," says Dr. Silver.

Ginny sits up a little straighter, though I'm pretty sure she is not the mental health professional Mr. and Mrs. Lovecraft would choose, as "court-appointed" and "free" are probably not on their list of requirements.

"So we're just supposed to wait until the girl remembers if there was a crime?" Detective Curley says, rolling his eyes.

"That is exactly what we mean," Lawyer Gene says, standing. "Vivienne has nothing else to say."

We take that as our cue to get our stuff.

"If you don't mind, I'd like to speak with Mr. Lovecraft alone for a moment," Detective Curley says from behind his desk, irritation replaced by something cooler.

Mrs. Lovecraft blinks crazily at Mr. Lovecraft. Lawyer Gene puffs up. "Anything you have to say to Henry Lovecraft you can say to me," he says, and there's a badass behind those wire-framed glasses.

"I gotta be honest, Lovecraft. I don't get why you're lawyering up over this." Detective Curley sounds like a TV cop. The others move into and down the hall, thick in conversation, and I stay behind, just outside the door, forgotten. I slide down to the floor and bury my face in my knees so no one walking by will bother me; unfamiliar crying kids scare people. Scooting closer gives me a good slant-view angle back into the room, where Lawyer Gene nods for Mr. Lovecraft to sit beside him.

"What's that supposed to mean?" says Mr. Lovecraft.

"I mean, this has got to be a public relations windfall.

You and your wife came under some heavy criticism after that girl disappeared. Some people called you negligent. 'Course it wasn't your fault the girl went missing: How could you have known? Still, some people didn't see it that way. Gotta hurt business, in a small city like this. But now: now you got a chance to be the hero. I'm just a dumb Boston detective, but it seems to me that this whole thing works out for you."

Suddenly I understand who Detective Curley is. When everyone else maybe forgot Vivienne Weir, Detective Curley is the guy who remembered. He's the guy who kept Vivi's photo taped inside his locker here at the station. The one who never felt the case get cold.

"Are you saying I waved a wand and made Vivienne Weir magically reappear?" Mr. Lovecraft is aggressive. Aggressive won't work with Curley. Lawyer Gene knows this and tries to calm things down.

"The detective isn't accusing you of anything. Are you, Detective?" says Lawyer Gene.

"I am not. And yet, you have your lawyer here," says Detective Curley. His chair squeals, and if the man had his feet up on his desk, I would not be surprised.

"Mr. Lovecraft and his wife have been through significant emotional trauma. It has taken years to get their lives back from a press that criticized them unfairly. Criticism, I would add, that would not have been heaped on them were they not public figures. Over the last seven years, they have grieved, they have prayed, and their prayers have been answered. Travis and Marie Weir were not alive to witness the miraculous return of their daughter. Let's not compound the tragedy by casting aspersions on the only family that Vivienne Weir has going forward," says Lawyer Gene.

The detective claps slowly.

Chairs scrape. Mr. Lovecraft and his lawyer are outta there, and so am I.

"Worth every penny you're paying him, Lovecraft," I hear the detective call as I make for the lobby, nearly seen by Mr. Lovecraft and Gene, and panting by the time I reach Mrs. Lovecraft and Ginny, without Harvey Silver, whose work here is done. The women sit on plastic chairs, and Ginny covers Mrs. Lovecraft's hands in her lap, as if she was the one traumatized.

"Oh! Vivi!" Mrs. Lovecraft says, surprised. "How did we lose you?"

Ginny pulls me down to sit in the chair on her other side. "There's something I need you to understand. No one is going to force you to remember something you aren't ready to. You have the Lovecrafts, and here at the precinct, I am your family." She pats my knee firmly. "You are not alone."

For the first time, I feel rotten for the way I've judged Ginny. She has holes inside her same as me, and she likes how I fill them. It just goes to show all anyone really wants is family.

. . . . .

This is the way you celebrate a win. This is life.

A napkin is draped in my lap and the fork I dropped is replaced before I can say *oops*. When I spill crumbs next to my plate, another waiter scrapes them away. The air conditioner gets turned down because the hostess saw me shiver from across the room, and then she checks to make sure I'm comfortable, twice. My Sprite is refilled without asking. In candlelight, everyone is prettier, and I am prettier, and it becomes a running joke that every time I stuff food in my mouth, someone will stop by the table to talk to the Lovecrafts and wish me well.

This is the treatment you get when you build things in this town.

My stomach is the only one not having a good time. It doesn't want to stretch, but I hear Wolf's warning that this could be over soon and a hibernation reflex is kicking in and I cannot stop eating this amazing, fancy, famous hotel-restaurant food. My gut gurgles, crying, "Enough!" for everyone to hear, and your parents laugh, and you laugh, and I hold my stomach, and though it will hurt to eat, I grab one more roll.

The laughter fades and arms cross over and between us, making our dirty plates vanish. Mrs. Lovecraft pushes a small box across the table to me. It's a shade of blue-green that I'd call big-money blue, and it's tied with white satin ribbon.

Mrs. Lovecraft runs two fingers along her collarbone, girly and excited. "Open it, Vivi."

"But it's so pretty, I'll ruin it."

"It's from Tiffany," you say flatly.

"Temple!" Mrs. Lovecraft protests. "Don't spoil it!"

"I'm just letting Vivi know the significance of the box. You want to open it, trust me," you say, and I hate that I'm missing something.

I look to Mr. Lovecraft—females look for his approval—and he nods, so I carefully untie the ribbon. Nestled on a square of cotton is a thick silver link bracelet with a single heart charm.

"Go ahead, read the heart," urges Mrs. Lovecraft.

I lift the charm. " 'Daughter,' " I read softly.

You've been quiet through dinner. True, we keep getting stares, and this likely does not play as cool at the Parkman School, and I have heard you complaining to your friends on your phone. I don't know how you feel about this silver heart, because you are their real daughter, and I'm just some girl from the past making your lives messy. Something hard flickers across your face, but then it's gone.

"Try it on," Mr. Lovecraft urges.

I try to slip it on, but my wrist is not as delicate as Mrs. Lovecraft imagined, and it pinches. Mrs. Lovecraft reaches across the table to help close it. As she does, she looks at my fingernails, and the corners of her mouth droop, and I'm aware of the white ridges from the lean year with Wolf.

I dangle the bracelet in the candlelight. "It's the most beautiful thing I've ever owned," I say, and this is true, and the way these people soften me is dangerous.

"We thought it would remind you of your place here with us. It's only going to get better from here on, we promise," says Mrs. Lovecraft. She looks to Mr. Lovecraft meaningfully.

He clears his throat and leans over his folded hands. "Vivi, we need to talk."

I drop my wrist and the bracelet clatters on the table. This is it. Time to drop Vivi Weir's skin.

I look for the nearest exit.

"Now I know we said one and done," Mr. Lovecraft says, "but there is another thing we can do to ensure the police don't continue to bring up unpleasant facts."

I'm wearing shoes I can't run in and that burner phone would have been handy right about now. I have been careless. I have gone soft as one of those dinner rolls, two of which could easily fit into my bag.

"It may seem frightening. But it's actually not as scary as it sounds."

Below the table, I drop a stolen dinner roll to the floor. "Scary?"

"The *Today Show* called," Mrs. Lovecraft blurts. "They'd like to do an interview."

"An interview? With who?"

"With you. Really, with us," Mrs. Lovecraft says, leaning toward me. "You wouldn't be alone, not for a minute."

"Why would they want that?" I say it slowly, like Vivi would, but really I'm just trying to calm my breathing down because I don't have to leave you. Yet.

"People care about you. You give them hope that sometimes, there are happy endings," Mrs. Lovecraft says.

"But won't it bring us more attention?" I say, attention being something I do not need.

"Actually, just the opposite," Mr. Lovecraft says, happy to correct me. "I have a public relations woman on my staff. She strongly recommends doing the interview. See, though we handled the police, the press won't leave us alone anytime soon. The *Today Show* is a one-shot deal, like ripping off a Band-Aid. It's the same principle as our conversation with Detective Curley. The press will have their story, and they'll leave us alone."

I think of that single reporter underneath my window. "There haven't been that many—"

"There's something else," he interjects. "Once the TV show airs and the public is behind us, the police will have more pressure on them to accept what you've told them."

"He means once the public is sympathetic to your story," Mrs. Lovecraft says.

There are a lot of things wrong with this idea. Instead, I blurt, "Two and done."

"Excuse me?" Mr. Lovecraft asks.

"It's not one and done anymore. It's two and done. This is the second thing," I explain.

"Oh, yes," Mrs. Lovecraft replies. "I suppose it is."

"Done is done," he says.

Here's the larger problem: the *Today Show* is on TV everywhere. Being on a national TV show is the equivalent of handing the Last One a piece of paper with my address on it. I'm not truly afraid the Last One will find and kill me. A con always looks for the angle that will benefit him most.

I'm afraid he will find and blackmail me.

"I am not going on the *Today Show*," you announce. "It would be supremely embarrassing."

"No need for you to come, darling," Mr. Lovecraft says, raising his palm. "This is about controlling Vivi's message."

"What Daddy means is that it would be a distraction from your activities. We can be down and back in the same day. It's only Manhattan," Mrs. Lovecraft says.

"No thank you," I say quietly.

They peer at me as though I just shrank.

"No thank you, as in you're not interested in doing the interview?" Mr. Lovecraft asks, with the faintest edge. I pull the bracelet into my lap, a knot in my throat. I have failed them, and they look disappointed. The weirdest part is, I actually care.

"Did they tell you this place is haunted?" you say suddenly.

This change of subject is its own kind of gift. "Haunted? By who?"

"A traveling liquor salesman who committed suicide in room 303. Guests say they can smell whiskey and hear laughter into the night," you say.

Mr. and Mrs. Lovecraft roll their eyes at each other, and the topic of morning news shows is dropped. They talk over us in code, and it's hard to listen in, because being the object of your laser focus is like being grass under a magnifying glass on a sunny day.

"And the elevator goes up to the third floor by itself, without anyone hitting the button," you say.

"Wow, really? Cool!" I sound naive, but it works because Vivi is the kind of girl who walks away with a kidnapper.

You stand. "I need to pee. Come with?"

"Same, yes." *And thank you.*

Mrs. Lovecraft studies us for a second. "Well, okay. Hurry back, though."

"Quick, before she changes her mind," you whisper. "We don't have much time!"

"To pee?"

"To see the haunted room. You said you wanted to."

I did?

"Follow me." You drag me into the chichi hotel lobby,

stealing past the clerk behind the desk and taking the stairs. We run, laughing, up three floors.

You stop on the third-floor landing. "Bwa-ha-ha-ha! Are you ready?"

Oh, Temple. There are scarier things in hotels than ghosts in rooms. Old men with bellies who have paid to meet you, for example.

"I'm ready."

We push the door open and prowl the hall, stealthy, and you are funny, making exaggerated hush signs and tiptoeing. You're corny, and it is cute, and you treat me like a dumb younger sister, and I sense that you're leading me into trouble but I am so okay with it, because trouble with you is fun, old-fashioned, clean fun, stealing poems and spotting ghosts, and I am charmed. We are Betsy and Tacy, Anne Shirley and Diana Barry, Nancy Drew and Bess Marvin. Come to think of it, we are the characters in all the books I ever stole and loved.

We pass room 302, then 304, and you turn to face me, frowning. "This is wrong. Where's 303?"

I study an unmarked door next to 305. "This has to be it."

"This can't be it. It's not a room," you say, sliding your palms together, like this is an emergency.

"It has to be. That's 302 and 304; this is 305, and that down there's 301," I say, pointing down the hall. "They must have boarded it up and taken the number down."

"They say you can smell whiskey and cigars. Can you smell anything?" you ask.

I lean into the door crack and sniff. "I smell ammonia. I think it's a utility closet."

"It's not a utility closet."

"Oh it's a utility closet. Maybe we'll come across a haunted janitor. That'd be scary. I can see an evil janitor— say with no face—haunting these halls at night. Can't you?"

"This is boring," you say, and if it weren't you, I'd snap back that it's boring because it's the kind of kicks ten-year-olds go for.

Instead, I say, "Your parents will worry. We should go."

The elevator dings and we turn as the gold doors open slowly. The down button is unlit, we are alone, and the compartment is empty.

I shake my finger at the empty car. "Okay, that was scary!"

"Wait, I know," you say, reaching in your back pocket

for your phone and dragging me inside. "I have a better idea." You hit *M*. *M* is for mezzanine, and this is where the lobby bar is, brass and leather and a piano even. You stride out as if we are *actually legal* and choose a high table for two at the edge, immediately dipping your head over the phone.

"We're going to get kicked out," I hiss.

You barely look up. "Meh. If you're rich enough to be here, no one cares."

"Who are you calling?"

"I'm not calling anyone. Okay, I'm sort of calling someone. Technically, I'm Tindering."

"You're what?"

You giggle, and I am getting angry but your giggle is sweet. You swipe right and bite your bottom lip. "Tindering. Calling any guy in a ten-mile radius who wants to hook up for sex."

"Why would you ever . . ." I'm shaking my head, dumbfounded. "Why would you ever do that?"

"Um, because it will be hilarious when they show up and it's you and me? And we can be like, um, we're here with our parents having dinner, and you must have got your wires crossed, sicko."

I shift in my seat. A waitress eyes us, wondering if

we'll try to order a drink, when in fact you just ordered a man.

"Relax," you say, picking at a bowl of sugared nuts. "I'm kidding. It doesn't work like that. Not exactly. You text the guy a few times first, make arrangements. I actually know him."

"You know him?"

"His name is Andrew."

"His name is Andrew?"

"You sound like a parrot. Mine's Tracy. It's fine. I told you, it's going to be hilarious when he sees how old I am."

"How old did you say you are?"

"Twenty-two. You only have to be eighteen."

"I just—God!" My chest is tightening and I'm starting to realize there is no convincing you of anything and you don't understand how dangerous men are and how can I protect you? "I mean, how long do you think we can even wait here? Your parents—"

Your eyes bulge at your phone. "He's here."

"What? Oh my God. Temple. Do not tell me he has a picture of you."

"Why do you think he came?"

I scan the room fast for Horny Andrew, and although a

lot of people in this showy bar look like they want some, I don't see a single guy scanning the room for a lanky honey-haired girl. Yet.

You shove your phone under my nose. "He's coming! Look, he's coming!"

A commotion across the mezzanine, and there are the Lovecrafts, followed by the manager on duty. They walk-run across the lobby to us. At the same time, a pudgy guy in a work suit appears behind you with an oily grin.

"Tracy?" he asks.

You grab your earlobe and gaze at him over your shoulder innocently. "I think you have the wrong girl."

"I don't think so. You're the girl in the picture," he says, leaning too close to you. "You know: Tinder?"

"Temple!" Mr. Lovecraft booms. Andrew's cheeks hit the floor, and if he peed his pants I would not be surprised, but there's no telling now, because he is beelining for the exit and you are already trying the innocent lobe-tugging thing on our father.

"Daddy, don't yell. We were just tired of that stuffy restaurant and came up here to people-watch."

"It looked more like you were getting picked up. I ought to go after that moron," Mr. Lovecraft says, and Mrs. Love-craft tugs on his arm.

"Come, Henry." She turns to thank the hotel manager in hushed tones and this dinner celebration is over.

The ride home is silent. The Lovecrafts' anger feels like a hair shirt, at least it is what I imagine it would feel like to wear one, maybe even to touch one. I am scared of what might come, but you are sulky and defiant, and it is glorious but also puzzling, because we really were wrong to freak your parents out like that. Dinner was over the top and my belly is nicely full, and we probably squeaked out of a sketchy if not dangerous scenario. Yet you sit the whole way home, stiff with anger, legs and arms crossed, staring out at the streaming lights reflecting off the Charles.

"I only did it to entertain Vivi," you say suddenly.

The Lovecrafts look sideways at each other across the front seat.

"She's safe with me. You both know that," you say, louder this time.

. . . . . .

I wake the next morning expecting to meet disapproval, or at least the cold shoulder. Instead, I meet Zack, my new tutor.

Zack Turpin is a Suffolk Law student in his early

twenties who seems to think I am mentally delayed, not just a little behind in school, and I have to show him, gently, that yes, I can do division and read beyond chapter books. The Lovecrafts want me to stick to the amnesia story with Zack, which is easier than explaining how I got books in the evil man's shed, so I say I don't remember how I learned things. It becomes clear quickly that though the Lovecrafts can afford what they want, they have not spent much money on Zack the law student, because he is working off lesson plans he downloaded from the Internet. I try not to care that they don't seem to think my schooling is equal in importance to yours, because it's a ridiculous thought, a jealous thought, a sibling-rivalry-ish thought, and why should I care? The day is long, but what I really mean is the day is long without you, and I didn't see you in the morning and now it is eight p.m. and I still have not seen you, and the Lovecrafts don't seem to mind much that you're hardly around.

I don't see you Tuesday either. Or Wednesday.

I hear you coming and going, but by the time I run downstairs or into the hall you are behind a closed door, or being driven somewhere. It's mostly just sleeping Slade and me, and I wonder why Slade never complains about how weird his job is. Then I realize that like me, Slade has no one but the girlfriend I hear him fighting with on his phone and the Lovecrafts. So he wants to serve the Love-crafts and doesn't care how strange their ideas are, because they are free with their love when someone fits in with their family.

I even begin to wish that Wolf will come, but of course he does not. I am deeply alone, and it is choking me.

When I finally catch up with you Thursday night, you seem angry. I play last Sunday's dinner at the restaurant over in my head, but sneaking off and making a fake Tin-der call wasn't my idea, so I can't figure out what I did wrong. I do know what I can do right, and it will be spec-tacular.

I wait until Friday night when the Lovecrafts are both out. Slade is already on duty, which I wasn't counting on. Luckily, he's absorbed, hunched over sexting his girlfriend at the Lovecrafts' kitchen counter. I approach your bedroom door and knock twice, softly. You don't answer, but I know you're in there, so I press the door open. You lie on your bed, head over the edge of the far end, legs on the wall, hair streaming over the headphones on your ears. I lift one earphone, and you jump.

"Jesus, Vivi!" you sputter, squirming and righting yourself, and you are a pretty spider, scrambling. "What the hell?"

I lay my finger to my lips. My turn. "Shh."

I toss your coat on the bed, along with a hat because I care.

You smile. No fear. Only interest. "Where are we going?"

"I have something to show you." I turn my back and check over my shoulder to see if you're following me to my room, and you are jamming your foot into an old Ugg boot, coat half hanging off. Game for anything. I smile to myself as I lift my window to a gust and climb onto my very handy fire escape. Your weight behind me makes the scaffolding shake, but I'm not scared, and I have yet to see you scared of anything.

On the ground, I face you, your features disappearing in my breath-bloom. "Are you okay with walking? It's not far."

"What direction?"

I point up Commonwealth Avenue, where we'll cut through Newbury to Boylston, and you push past me, and I'm forced to jog to keep ahead of you. As we walk, I try my tricks for not feeling the nighttime cold, from jamming my arms close to my body to pressing my lips together to hitting my feet hard on the ground to get the blood back in. You, on the other hand, walk so loose and easy. Anyone watching could tell who's the street kid from Florida and who's the private-school girl from this cold, cold town. It takes us half the time I figured it would to walk to our destination underneath the red, block-letter STEINWAY sign and the musical curlicue *S* beside it.

"Isn't it a little late at night to be shopping for pianos?" you yell over the wind.

I grab your wrist and pull you to the door, which is open on Friday nights because of the writers' group that has classes in the building. We push through and make our way to the elevator. As we walk by the darkened piano show-room on the first floor, you say under your breath, "So we aren't buying a piano." The elevator has a metal gate inside that I have to drag hard to shut.

Your hand hovers near the buttons. "Going up?"

"Down," I say.

You raise your eyebrows and hit the basement button, and the elevator lurches so hard we fall into each other, laughing. After a long time—forty feet underground, but I let you wonder—we hit the basement floor with a bang.

I lead the way into the dark, nailed by the ammonia smell of rat droppings, feeling for the lightbulb socket hanging from a cord on the ceiling. I twist the bulb.

"What's your plan now, mysterious?" you say, smiling as the light reveals the padlocked door in front of us.

I push the wooden crate Wolf and I use to reach the top rail over the door. The key takes a while to find in the dust. When I feel it, I jump down and get busy on the lock, pretending not to notice that you're nodding, impressed. The key is stiff in the padlock, and I work it hard until it gives a satisfying *pop*. I ease the door open and flick on the row of light switches, one at a time, slow for effect, *tick, tick, tick, tick, tick, tick*. The lights come up and we are standing in front of a faded mural of ancient Romans or maybe Greeks—I never know—in togas. I take your elbow and turn you around.

"What is this?" you gasp.

"This is Steinert Hall," I say, twirling around a pillar, white paint flaking under my hand. "It hasn't been used since 1942."

Your chin tips up the way mine was at the Pops. "That's the same year as the Cocoanut Grove fire," you murmur at the round ceiling.

"What fire?" I say.

140

"A nightclub fire. It happened that same year across town. People blamed a busboy who threw a match that lit a fake palm tree. It spread to the fabric on the ceiling." You walk to the center of the hall and shade your eyes, gazing up at the balconies that encircle us. "Showered the people below in sparks. Most died from the fumes, actually. Or they were trampled at the revolving door. Four hundred and ninety-two in all."

I whistle and it echoes through the space.

You point to painted letters and arrows on the walls on either side of me. "To Carver Street, that way," you read. "To Boylston Street, that way."

I look above my head to where the marble staircase exits are boarded over. "Not anymore," I say.

"Right. We're, what, thirty feet underground?"

"Something like that," I say.

You walk up the aisle and up some stairs to a fine old chair on the stage. "It's beautiful," you say, stroking your fingers along its back. "How did you know about this place?"

I pretend to study the swirly wrought-iron pattern that frames the stairs. "We all have our secrets," I say, but I'm thinking that sometimes, homeless people get caught jumping the turnstiles at the Park Street station and they have miles to go before they sleep, and that chair you're so fond of is better than the pavement under the awning of the burrito place next door.

"Mmm," you say, taking in the view. "This is some stage."

"It was built by the guys who started the piano store above. Used to seat six hundred fifty people. The coosticks are supposed to be perfect."

"A-coustics," you murmur, gazing up at the empty balcony.

I wince. I may have gotten the word wrong, but I know what it means. "So, test it out."

Your head snaps. "What do you mean?"

"I mean you should sing."

You fiddle with your sleeves. "I can't. You know that."

"It doesn't have to be perfect. I won't even listen. Look, I'm blocking my ears." I cover my ears.

You bite your lip.

"Do you want me to leave?" I ask.

You turn from me, one hand on the back of the chair. I step out of the room and pretend to close the door, balling up a tissue from my pocket and sticking it into the lock hole quick—an old trick so that I can open it silently, and after a minute, I do. Through the crack, I see you close your eyes and plant your feet. Your hand rises to rest on your chest.

You open your eyes and focus on the pile of broken pianos at the back of the hall. Finally, the sound comes, low and sweet, a song about a world of pure imagination.

It's a song I've heard before, from a movie made long ago: old-fashioned, Technicolor, with a chocolate waterfall and a girl who turns into a blueberry and explodes. And it has nothing to do with chocolate or blueberries. You're singing to me. Telling me life with you is freedom and I have chosen well.

You finish the last note and cover your face with your long white hands. I pull the door shut softly and wait for you to come to me.

. . . . .

The next night, sleep comes in dark waves. I've felt better about us since you sang to me, though I've seen little of you in the day since. It's past midnight when I jolt awake. I wait a minute, hearing nothing but my own ragged breathing, but the air is disturbed. I feel under my pillow for the knife and touch the cold handle when you whisper near my ear, "Time to go!"

I am dragged from bed and dressed in your clothes, clothes I can't see. I don't struggle. It feels like a dream, to have your hands on me, fingers tugging at a zipper, buttoning the fly at my waist.

"God, it's like dressing an infant! A little help, please," you whisper.

"Where have you been?" I murmur sleepily, swaying.

"Does it matter?" you hiss. "And be quieter if you want to come. Slade's job is to watch me. Most nights he stares at porn in his room, but you never know when he might get bored."

You pull the nightshirt over my head and the shock jars me awake, a sudden arousal. You hand me my bra.

"This one's your job," you say.

I twist into the bra and the shirt you hand me and like that you are gone, one leg thrown through the window, and we are getting good at this. We launch ourselves into the night and onto the shaky fire escape. This time I follow your dark shape, led only by the pale flashes of your miniskirted legs. From the last landing we leap to the alley, noisily, and I hope Slade's skin flick has a good story line.

"Come, down here," you say, dragging me to the corner of Comm Ave., away from the brownstone. Your phone glows in your hand; you've already called for a car.

"Where are we going?"

"You'll see."

The car arrives, and a guy with a slick smile leans over the passenger seat and buzzes down his window. "Tempull?" he asks.

"Tell me where we're going or I won't come," I say.

You laugh and slide into the car. "We both know that's not going to happen."

I wait outside the car, door hanging open, rubbing my shoulders. By the light of the car door I see what I'm wearing. The jeans are skinny and the shirt is cropped just under my chest. It is not my best combination. You bend close to a lighted compact, slicking on lipstick.

My hand floats to the back of my neck.

"You have bedhead. It's fine. It works," you say without looking at me. "Get. In."

"Works for what?" I say.

"Where we're going," you say.

I blow my cheeks out in a raspberry and slide in beside you. The phone on the driver's clip-on stand says we are driving to Somerville, outside the Back Bay and a world away. I know this because Keloid Kurt was from Somerville. Called himself one of the last remaining members of the Winter Hill Gang. No one listened. He grumbled constantly about the "Yuppies" and "gen-a-fecation" and only shut up after someone ate his rat. The driver gets lost and you lose your patience. He tries to let us out in the middle of nowhere, but you say there's no chance he's dumping and running, you'll give him a lousy rating and post a complaint. Finally he takes another turn and we land in front of a warehouse thumping with music, and you do tiny baby claps. We scramble out of the car. You make nice with the driver, ask him if he might come back in a few hours. He makes a crude noise and speeds off. I say something about taking the train, and you look at me like I'm crazy.

"The train stopped two hours ago," you say, opening the door to the warehouse.

I am not a fan of EDM—it gives me a headache—and I wouldn't have thought you were, either, with your fancy opera training. We are way young for this crowd, and I wouldn't be concerned except you've got me breaking every one of my survival rules. Don't wear clothes that show off your body, for starters. But maybe I'm wrong, because no one is sizing us up: no one is even paying attention to us, not really. This crowd is here for the DJ, who stands on a second level, and they look up to him like he is a god, jumping, dancing, shuffling, waving their hands. This is a neon rave, and these are throwbacks, kandi kids and not-so-young kids, and for sure, lots of people here are on something, but this is a happy crowd. You grab my arms and drag me to the front row. The music booms, its pulse in my ears and veins. It feels like something is trying to punch its way out of my throat. You start dancing and I am awkward. Then I close my eyes and let go.

This is exactly what I needed. A familiar heat builds inside me, a heat I'm liking. A heat I don't want to release just yet.

An out-of-place-looking guy watches us. He is older, hooded. He stands behind us, too close, until we both stop dancing and back away. He swoops fast and whispers something in your ear, and the urge to grab your arm and run is strong. You dig in your pocket and pass him a wad of cash, and he places something in your hand. You turn and show me two beige tablets printed with the letter *M*.

"We don't need it," I mouth.

You smile as if you don't understand me and shrug, popping both. I try to pretend you didn't just do that, try not to worry that you have no idea what was in them, and dance, but honestly, it's ruined for me. Rich kids think drugs make them edgy, when the opposite is true: it just makes them dull. I want to leave the front line, but I'm crushed by bodies, and twenty minutes later you abandon the shuffle moves everyone else is doing for grinding on guys, and then the beat changes, and you're hanging on me. I know you're playing, but soon I'm swept up in it, too: the pounding bass, the flashing lights, the neon. No one cares what I look like out here: it's just us, and you seem fine, maybe it was filler in the pills.

You reach for my arm but miss as you dive toward the sawdust floor. I yank you upright before you hit it. You're pale and sweaty. I throw your arm over my shoulder and shove people aside, and people are pissed, and I don't care, because you're giving me nothing, no help, you're so weak, and I need to get you out of this place but I can't find the door we came in. When I see people with water bottles, I realize we have been dancing for hours with nothing to drink. Finally, I spot the exit sign and push through the door, leaning you against a cement wall.

"So thirsty," you gasp.

I jab my finger in your face. "Stay here. Do you understand me? Stay. Here."

I walk among packs of people, mostly having cigarettes, and I beg but no one has water to share, and someone does have a beer, and that'll do. I bring the beer over and you accept it gratefully. I consider taking a sip myself, but I should save it for you.

Your pupils are fat olives. "I love you for saving me," you say, licking your dry lips and holding the beer in both hands like a mug of something warm.

"I didn't save you," I say. "We need to get home. Tell me your phone still has juice."

You look at me as though I have proposed the most brilliant idea, and fish in the pocket of your mini, which in addition to you looking so vulnerable is getting us unwanted attention. We need to move, soon. You pull the phone out and hit the car service app.

"I hope it will find us," you say weakly.

You hope. I am thinking of the Lovecrafts' disappointment when we vanished from the dinner table. What will happen if they realize we're not in our beds?

"You look so sad," you murmur, moving a chunk of sweaty hair from my eye. "What are you thinking about?"

"How much trouble we're going to be in if your parents find out," I say.

You laugh, at first weakly, then it spreads to your belly and grows into something hyena-pitched and hysterical. Two large bald dudes are checking you out and I wish you would stop.

"It's not funny," I hiss.

You ignore me and twirl, looking up at the sky and

talking about the stars, how they look like frosting, and you love doing Molly, because you feel things you can't normally feel, and you wished I'd done it, too, because friendship is about sharing, and we are new friends, and I don't bother correcting you by reminding you that we are old friends.

"If your parents find out we came to a rave, they could send me away," I insist.

You stop twirling and stagger for a moment, then swoop toward me, taking my face in your hands. Underneath, my cheeks flame. "Oh sweet, dumb Vivi. They'll never let you get away."

We are framed in a car's headlights, and you check the license plate to your phone. Satisfied, you climb in. To my surprise, a potbellied woman busting out of a Coachella T-shirt climbs into the front seat, and when I say, "Hey," thinking she's stealing our ride, you say, "Carpool," and that explains it. The driver cranks the air conditioner aggressively, and my sweat is drying. I shiver. You collapse and draw your knees up, head in my lap, smiling up at me dreamily.

"You have the most beautiful skin. Like melted coffee ice cream," you say.

The lady in the front seat sneaks a look and snickers. I look out the window, embarrassed.

You sit up suddenly and twist toward the door, palm against the window.

"I feel sick," you whisper.

"Pull over!" I scream. The driver's eyes flash in the mirror and he swings to the curb. "Get her out!" he yells. You get out on the empty street and I slide out behind as you dry-heave into a bush. I hold your hair and stroke your back and remind you that you are dehydrated, and call to the driver, asking if he has water. He shakes his head disgustedly and gets out to check if you puked in the backseat. The car door alarm chirps, a shrill *ding, ding, ding.*

"Are you okay?" I murmur, rubbing your back.

You nod gratefully. "So much better."

The lady in the front seat yells to the driver, "Leave the hoes!"

You straighten. "What did you say?"

The lady hangs out of the passenger seat and pokes her taffy hair out the window. "I said, we should leave you, hoes!"

You charge at her. I try to catch you, but you're already on top of taffy hair in the front seat, pummeling her lumpy arms with your fists. The driver hops up and down and threatens to call the cops. You manage to drag the woman out of the passenger seat and hurl her to the ground.

I grab your wallet off the seat and throw a ring of bills at the driver, crying, "You'll drive when I say drive!" Only after I see his shocked face do I realize the bills are hundreds. I scramble back to the street and grab you, now kicking the woman in her ribs, by your waist and throw you in the car, still kicking.

The driver screeches away from the woman.

"You say she started it! That is why I left her!" he warns over the front seat, and I promise we will. I try to soothe you, but you're glaring out the window, itching for more action.

Finally, you turn to face me. Your look is too intense and I wish you'd speak.

"I guess you crashed?" I say, trying to make light. Your dead seriousness scares me.

"I call it my bloodlust. The sensation of hitting, pummeling, crushing. I crave it sometimes."

"How often is sometimes?"

"Only when I witness something unfair."

"I see."

"You're the same, you and me. I can tell. A natural-born killer," you say and laugh darkly. You lie back down in my lap and become gentle again, and I love seeing you framed like this, hair all around, the heat of your head.

"Only when there's a right to wrong," I kid.

You waggle your finger at me. "See? We're cut from the same cloth. I knew the first moment I saw you."

"When we were little?" I say.

"Mmmm." You seem to fall asleep. In the half-light, your face is damp and feverish. When I am sure you're passed out, I blow lightly across your face. You smile with closed eyes.

We wind down Memorial Drive and across the Mass Avenue bridge in the predawn glow. At a stoplight, I watch as a mother and her kid step out of a bus, so painfully early, the kid begging to be carried. The mother is young but life has worn her face. I imagine she is taking her daughter to a place where she'll pay to have her babysat while she works for that same money. She carries a vacuum cleaner. The daughter's starfish hands reach up, and the mother drops the vacuum and meets her daughter's hands, swinging her side to side, mustering sweet, tired words.

Inside me, the old rage puckers and releases. Biding its time.

· · · · ·

You crave risk and you crave bloodlust. I crave protection and I crave you. Nine days have passed without you. The excuses range from rehearsals to weekends at friends' vacation homes to tutoring sessions, and I am busy with Zack, too, but he leaves at two o'clock and then—that is, now—there is nothing. I am as underscheduled as you are overscheduled, and the Lovecrafts seem determined to find even more things to keep you busy. I am left alone for entire afternoons just like this, my saddest hours, though I am always happy to shed Zack. I have taken to wandering, watched by the plaster angels. Old habits are hard to break, and so far I have tallied about seventy thousand dollars of stuff worth stealing.

Yet I will not steal, because that would be stupid, but also because Mrs. Lovecraft's kindnesses have pried open the fist I've made of myself. She opens me up in other ways, too. Everywhere, I see mothers. In the growing belly of the housecleaner. In the waiting room at the dentist Mrs. Lovecraft takes me to. On the streets of Boston, pushing strollers that look like drones. Everywhere, mothers tending to daughters. I begin to remember. The sounds in the tiny house where I was born. Its shade of French's mustard, what Momma called a happy color. Where the front door was always open to let God's air-conditioning come in. Momma's boyfriend then, a good man named Jackson who worked two jobs and drove a Chevy Impala and swung Momma around every time she walked in the door. Then later, the Impala and Momma's old self gone, and the apartments in Jasper, Homestead, Blountstown, and the last one in Immokalee, as we worked our way closer to the casinos, where marks grew like kudzu.

Mrs. Lovecraft and I talk a lot about how one little event can change the course of someone's life, and it's like she knows about Momma, and the person she was, and what our life was like before she met the Last One buying butts at the Timesaver. He told her he drove Everglades tours for an airboat company, but driving isn't the same as casting the ladies' lines and gutting their catches and keeping the beer on ice for tips. The Last One saw something in Momma, something actressy that liked to perform. More importantly, he saw a little seed of anger at the world for not treating her right, something he could grow. She saw something in him, too. He was a preacher and a teacher. He railed against the dangers of doing drugs, and as the dealer who didn't use, she thought him a model of self-restraint, given her own weaknesses for anything that numbed her. As a teacher, he brought her game up to a whole new level. They'd pretend to be that local couple in the bar at the fancy Chart House, charming the tourists with lies about his time in the Coast Guard and wrestling gators. People would invite them to dinner, and they'd skip out on their share of the bill. That sort of thing. Pretty soon they got known in Belle Glade and we had to leave the happy house behind. Around the time we moved on, the Last One began to notice my potential. By the time I turned fourteen, I'd gone to five schools, answered to five different names, and driven a getaway car.

Driving the getaway car was unplanned. Momma was the shill and we had no one else to drive. It was a short con gone bad: I don't remember the details. Around the time we got to Immokalee, we'd done so many cons, flimflams, grifts and gaffs, they started to blur.

What I do remember about Immokalee: tears. Bus tickets. A stash of money in the cookie tin. A packed suitcase under the bed. Momma getting ready to leave him.

Your absence drives me to these sad thoughts. Wears me down, day after day.

Mrs. Lovecraft doesn't like to interrupt my tutoring sessions and never sticks around. Slade is unconscious. I wander into Mr. Lovecraft's office and slide the pocket door closed behind me. A dark drizzle blurs the windows and reduces the sidewalk people to their brightest colors. The restaurant is closed now, but I stare anyway, the way Mr. Lovecraft did that first night I came, wondering what he saw. Himself and herself, I imagine, having dinner, never suspecting someone would break in and disrespect the safety that comes with being rich, and take their daughter's friend.

For the first time, I wonder: Why not you? You had to be a tempting morsel for a baby twiddler, that dimpled chin and those pretty eyes. The Lovecrafts were lucky. Lucky people born to a world of near misses and fortunes. Looks. Power. Children so spectacular they scare their own parents.

Mr. Lovecraft's desk is very old and glossy and has lots of little cubbies. I sit in the leather chair and lean back, pretending to be a man of importance. I wonder what a man of importance earns each year.

I slide open a drawer.

A fat packet of glossy pages are held together with a black clip. I have stumbled upon Henry Lovecraft's personal version of porn: a collection of stories featuring himself. There are *Boston* magazine articles and *Yale Alumni Magazine* articles and look, even a whole *People* magazine containing an interview he and Mrs. Lovecraft did after Vivi disappeared. They are not the cover story; a little box in the corner has a picture of me. I separate the packet into two neat piles and turn to the article. A warm flush fills my cheeks as I look at the Lovecrafts from seven years ago. They are smoother around the eyes and mouth, with larger pupils and lusher hair. His hand grips her shoulder and he stands behind her. Their eyes are guarded: they are under attack, and this is their chance to tell their side of the story.

I slip the magazine back. I know this story already: it is mine. Underneath Henry's porn is another fat packet, this time clippings of his only daughter's achievements, including the profile I read in the library. I lift it out and glance through the stories, and that's just what they are: stories. They have nothing in common with the Temple I am growing to know, the Temple who feels like a marionette on strings. The Temple who insists the perception of the golden child is not the reality. Only I know this Temple. This is the Temple you save for me. My lap grows warm, thinking of your head there, those grateful eyes, the vulnerability. I'm the best thing to come along to you in all of ever. I am your release valve, the friend who knows you from before, but not now. Who has no expectations of what you should be. You can be anything with me, Temple, and I will accept you and cherish you. Where others see an overachieving straight arrow I know a pervert with a thing for EDM, Molly, and freaky puppets. I specialize in damaged things and you don't need to be fixed, you need your spiky parts arrayed like the deadly sun that you are. You can't touch a sparkler, you have to hold it at arm's length, let it blaze and appreciate its beauty.

I get you, Temple. I get you.

A siren starts and I jump, falling forward slightly, and my fingers press the drawer bottom. It springs back against my fingertips, and a false bottom pops up. I slip my fingernails underneath as the front door slams shut.

"Vivi!" you call from the front door, urgent. You want me. I wait until your calls move upstairs and into my bedroom before I slip out of the office and onto the parlor couch, pretending to be asleep.

. . . . .

Of course you like cemeteries.

I suppose a girl whose best friend disappeared when she was nine years old might be hung up on the possibility of death. I will give you this. But chilling at King's Chapel Burying Ground as the sun goes down has to be among the creepier things I've done (and that's saying a lot). It's the oldest cemetery in Boston, and the kind of place that likes to remind you that you, too, are going to die, its gravestones carved with winged death's-heads flying to heaven, and hourglasses with shifting sands.

You lie on the grave of Joseph Tapping. It's carved with a face-off between a bearded Father Time and Death. Your knees are bent, because in olden times people were short, or maybe just the graves were. It's not a nice thought.

"I guess old Joseph Tapping wanted more time?" I say.

Your hands are folded behind your head and your elbows point outward and you look uniquely relaxed. I can't bring myself to lie on a grave, so I lean against one, and it is ridiculous that no one's kicking us out for disrespecting this historic place, but this seems to be a theme with you, a girl who defies correction in any form.

"Hmm?"

"Father Time and the skeleton facing off. You know: the struggle between life and death?"

"I never thought about it."

"Temple, why are we here?"

"Because when my parents ask where we were and you feel the overwhelming need to be truthful, you will tell them we went to an ancient graveyard, and they will be completely freaked out."

She really believes I am a dork. "You want to freak them out."

"I do. And thank you in advance for that," you say, and, out of nowhere, "I'm not afraid of dying."

This surprises me less than the fact that we are hanging out at a cemetery. "Huh."

"It's different for you, I suppose," you say.

"Maybe we shouldn't talk about it," I say.

"Right you are. Henry and Clarissa's mandate: gotta practice not-remembering." You smile at the sky, and this makes me smile. A normal sixteen-year-old would be tip-toeing around my special status, but you're so funny about it, and then so sarcastic about your parents' warped plan, which smacks of self-preservation (which, as long as it works for me, whatev).

If only I didn't have to act like mousy Vivienne, you and I would take on the world.

"What are you thinking about?" you ask, but you don't really want to know, because it's that drawer with its false bottom.

I go with innocent and stupid. "How life is short and we should make the most of it."

"Sounds like you got the message. Do you know what I'm skipping right now?"

"I knew you had to be skipping something to have dragged me here. Cello?"

"Wrong."

"Fencing?"

"That's tomorrow."

"Math Team?"

"Nothing. The answer's nothing. Because I quit French Club, which is what this hour is—was—dedicated to. My parents don't know, and I'm not telling them. In fact, I'm going to keep quitting things until they find out. And when that happens, it's going to be epic."

Oh, Temple. You rebel by quitting "extracurriculars" and, well, yes: stealing poems and Tindering, and taking the occasional party drug. I rebelled by telling Momma's boyfriends I had bugs "down there" so they would leave me alone. Still, we are cut from one cloth, and even if you think I'm bland Vivi, you also know we are the same, some-where deep and sweet.

You pat the ground next to me. "Sit."

I obey.

"Do you remember how we used to tell people we were triplets, but we ate our sister in the womb?" you ask.

I flutter-blink before answering. "Yeah, of course. It's so funny you remember that."

"We were impossible. We refused to be apart, remem-ber? We had to wear the same color to school, and chalk our hair, and bring the same exact snacks in our lunch boxes. For the whole month. My mother was a bitch about it, but your mother was *sooo* patient. I'm not making you sad talking about your mom, am I?"

"No," I say, burying my head in my knees.

"I can tell you have a hole inside, where your mother was. And I'm sorry for that. I'm really, really sorry."

You don't even know, Temple Lovecraft.

But you do know, because you rise and hug me. "I know I'm awkward," you say into my hair. "I say awkward, awful things. It's just—"

You pull away. Don't pull away, not yet. Blood pumping to the farther parts. Heat.

"I always wished I had your mom instead of mine. She laughed at everything we did; she didn't freak about anything."

I press my lips together in a pained smile. This would pain Vivi, and it pains me.

"Like that time after school when she let us butter the cat."

Whose cat? My cat? The Lovecrafts' cat? Did they have a cat? Don't panic.

You shake your head slowly. "So wrong and so awesome. It was almost better than the time she let us use your bike air pump to blow up tomatoes. It was spectacular! Little seeds in our hair and on our clothes. We called it our 'science homework.' I still have the urge to explode a tomato sometimes."

I force a grunt that could mean anything.

"Oh my God. Remember spying on the couple who lived two doors down? They always had their shades open and you could see right in from my window seat on the second floor? They were nudists, basically!"

"Basically."

"We were terrors. Remember how mad your dad got when we made signs saying 'Sorry for the damage to your car' and left them on cars parked on Comm Ave.?"

Remember? Remember? I do not remember, and I cannot pretend to remember, because I never did anything like this. I've been a working girl my whole life. My after-school activities consisted of stalking cars at stoplights wearing an orange vest and begging for change in my pail marked FOR THE CHILDREN. My version of spying involved hanging around ATMs watching people key in their pins and memorizing them for later when I stole the cards. I did my actual science homework lying across hotel room bedspreads waiting for online "dates" to arrive. I did not have leisure time to do Stupid Kid

Stuff. Period. And right about now I'm feeling pretty bad about it.

"We were crazy," I say. It sounds lame. I am lame. Maybe I'm reminding you how lame Vivi actually was. This afternoon is going wrong in so many directions I've lost track, and man, it's getting dark in this cemetery. I suddenly stand, because this walk down memory lane and these opportunities for getting caught are bugging me out. "I'm super cold."

You stand too, brushing off your back and your jeans. A leaf is caught in your hair, and I want so badly to pluck it out, but it seems intimate and wrong, because so far, you have done the touching.

"I'm never cold. Or I feel nothing. I think that's changing, though." You dissolve into laughter. "That sounded like a seriously crappy song lyric."

I smile. "I get it."

"Yeah?"

"Yeah."

We stroll through the lines of crumbling graves, taking our time, safe to say what we want among the dead forgotten.

"I lied before," you say. "We're not here just because I like to freak my parents out. I like cemeteries because they remind me that I'm mortal. That I have to die like every other person. Memento mori."

"So slow down and enjoy," I say.

"Something like that," you say.

"Memento mori. It's our new motto," I say, liking the way us having a motto sounds.

You stop at the gate and face me. Behind you, people rush to catch the train, on a different track than us, in a different world, operating at a different speed.

"But it doesn't work for you. I would think you'd want to rush forward with your life now that things are better."

I know exactly what to say. Thank you, gods, for giving me this chance to be the one to do the touching. I move your hair over your shoulder. "Actually, it's totally the opposite. I'm appreciating everything I have now so much more." For this moment, I let myself get lost in the things I wish to see, the clear eyes and the pillowy lips and the doll cheeks, and forget the false desk drawer that holds what I do not.

· · · · ·

A moment is an exact point in time and by definition it does not last.

I tell myself this as I stand, paralyzed, at the door to Mr. Lovecraft's office, hours after Mr. Lovecraft has left for work, Temple has gone to school, and Mrs. Lovecraft drifted away on vague errands. The secret drawer calls to me, and I dread what it might contain. Memento mori. Slow down and enjoy, Jo. Don't be in a rush to see things that could change everything.

I have an actual excuse that has nothing to do with my fear of what's in that envelope. There is Slade, inexplicably awake and parked outside the window of Mr. Lovecraft's office. His SUV sits at the curb, running. Because the dummy can't find one of the Lovecrafts' chargers, he's destroying the ozone layer so he can argue with his girlfriend. He pops a vein as he yells and this will not end well, and it will not end soon, and is seemingly worth losing his sleep over. Across the Common, a meter maid tickets cars. It will take her a while to reach Slade, but she will reach him, and this fight is a doozy, one that means plenty of hate-sex later.

The good con isn't afraid of information. Also: the good con manages the unexpected.

I drop to my knees and crawl to the office window, catching the cord to the blinds and easing them closed an inch. It is a lightless afternoon made darker by all this wood. Don't notice the shades have closed partway, Slade, don't look. Focus on saying cruel things to your girlfriend. My fingers press the false bottom of the drawer and its floor pops. I place the false bottom aside.

Inside is a yellow envelope tied with red string.

A honk, a terrible, endless blast. I lift a slat and peek through. Slade has dropped his head over the steering wheel and smacked the horn. This is the end of his fight or added drama. Either way, my time is short. A stamp in the corner reads *Forlizzi & Associates Private Detective Agency.*

Leave it. Replace the false floor, close the drawer, and don't look back.

Except I am alone now, and I don't have to be Vivi. I can be Jo, whose sticky fingers would be in that envelope already. Open the envelope, Jo.

Mr. Lovecraft's trinkets glare at me. A brass mastiff, a helicopter paperweight, and a Tom Brady bobblehead, things fondled by him and dusted by the cleaners. *Ungrateful girl*, they say. *Untrusting.*

The envelope, Jo.

I unwind the string from the envelope and dump the contents on the desk.

Papers slip and fall from my fingers, clumsy from shock. I am looking at my life.

. . . . .

On the desk, I feather a packet of research on Jolene Chastain. More accurately, on Patrice Chastain. Here we have arrest records. Here we have citations for vagrancy. For loitering. For panhandling. Mug shots. Momma, her hair oily, eyes glassed. Not a trail of Jolene, not a footprint, because I am a minor, but that doesn't make a difference. The Lovecrafts know who I am.

My knees shake, and from the sound of it, a meter maid is knocking on Slade's window. I gather the papers in my arms and drop to the floor, crawling to lean against the wall, the world beyond my eyes gone white and staticky. At the edges of the fuzz I hear Slade, muffled arguing that echoes from miles away. The fuzz recedes, but the electricity remains. Mr. and Mrs. Lovecraft suspected I wasn't Vivienne Weir and paid someone to confirm it. For weeks, they've only been pretending that I'm her.

My cheeks drop, cold with horror.

If they know I'm not Vivienne Weir, do you know, too?

A car door slams. I gather the papers and jam everything back into the drawer, messy, but there's no time to escape, because Slade probably runs up stairs as part of his regular training, though he will be dejected and maybe slower. Sitting in Mr. Lovecraft's chair would not be cool, so I stand, staring out the half-closed blinds as though it is natural and the view is fascinating. I feel Slade stop in the door frame. He wants to say something, but he senses I am having a moment and is afraid to interrupt.

"Miss Weir?" he says.

"Yes, Slade?" I reply, tilting to give him even more of my back.

"Everything okay?" he asks.

"I should ask you the same. How come you're awake?"

He shifts, hands jammed in pockets. "Sometimes I have business. Things I need to stay awake for." He is wondering how much I saw or heard, and how much of that I am willing to share with the Lovecrafts. There has to be some kind of behavior clause people like the Lovecrafts make people like Slade sign.

I know what I must do. I've seen him run nonsense errands for you more than once—a Frappuccino, a run to the Apple store to fix your cracked screen. "Actually, I'm not okay. I really need an Advil. The Lovecrafts don't have any in their medicine cabinet. Could you run to the CVS on Newbury for me?"

"You want me to go for you?" he asks, caveman-style.

"I'd go, but the Lovecrafts don't want me going out alone. For a while, I guess. Until everything dies down."

He rests his knuckles on his wide hips and straightens to his full height. "That's not going to work, Miss Weir. You can't leave, and I can't leave, either. Not unless there's a specific change in protocol."

"Protocol?"

"Yeah."

"How long did you serve before you started doing private security?"

Slade shuffles his feet. "I went Blackwater before I went PSD after ten months in Iraq."

He stares at those shuffling feet as he says this, and although I have loads of respect for our soldiers, I do not have time to ask Slade to explain his acronyms, or to be sensitive to his reasons for not managing to stay in the army. Because I now know the Lovecrafts aren't paying him to protect me. They're paying him to keep me here. And the time has come to leave.

"Okay, then I think I'll go lie down."

I grab a canvas shopping bag on my way up the stairs, groping the rail like I'm blinded by a headache. When I reach the top, I peek down. Slade is hammering at his phone, planning his makeup sex. And if I'm right, Mrs. Lovecraft is going to walk through that door anytime during the next hour. I slam my bedroom door for Slade's benefit and head straight down to Mr. and Mrs. Lovecraft's bedroom, a pretty place of calm greens and creams. This is one of my favorite rooms in the whole house, the bedroom Wolf and I would have if we were really a couple, but there is no time for daydreaming and I have a cruise to pack for. The *Vendeem* leaves Boston Harbor every Wednesday from May through August for Montreal. I have known this since I became Vivi Weir, and this is my escape. The tiny safe in this room is no use to me, since I ran out of time to learn the code. I take what I can take, which is limited to Clarissa's pearls, the tacky Rolex Mr. Lovecraft never wears, and a wad of Clarissa's "mad money" she keeps stuffed in her bra drawer. I head back upstairs to your room. It is dark and I leave it dark, ashamed to let your things see me. You keep your new laptop on the desk you never use. It's worth at least $899. I slip it in the sack, which sucks for this purpose, and it also sucks for holding a tennis racket, but I throw it in anyway. Your diamond earrings are pushed through a ceramic jewelry tree. I whisper "I'm sorry" as I unscrew the backs and tuck them in my pocket. I move toward a vanity table with drawers made to hide tiny expensive things, and there are frames with pictures of Vivi that I've seen but never studied. You and Vivi next to a big, bronze teddy bear sculpture in front of a fancy toy store. You and Vivi on a picnic blanket with the Esplanade's Hatch Shell in the background: Fourth of July, some year. Vivi's third-grade class picture. Vivi cut out of your class picture, in a frame. Black-and-white Vivi eating free Ben & Jerry's on National Ice Cream Day in an article in a newspaper called *Back Bay Windows*. I guess a shrine to Vivi is understandable. But the pictures of Vivi, right next door to where the real Vivi is supposed to be lying in bed? The opportunities for physical comparison day after day freak me out. I'm leaving not a moment too soon.

Downstairs, a door slams meaningfully. This is not the habit of elegant Mrs. Lovecraft, or even powerful Mr. Lovecraft, who saves his drama for the boardroom. I hear the muted jawing of Slade, and I need to get into my bedroom fast and hide this stuff or I am screwed. The bag swings and I wince as the laptop knocks into the door, but you are opening the fridge and slamming around and can't hear me hiding a stolen stash under my bed. Your footsteps fly up the stairs, sounds like gunfire, and you explode in, wearing your school uniform, cheeks aflame, tears streaming. You throw back your head and scream, a sound that starts low and climbs higher and higher until I block my ears. It's the scream of an animal injured. Then it is over, and you are holding your jaw.

"Temple," I whisper. "What the heck?"

"Ansel Carter is a beast!" you rasp, fingers around your throat now, massaging wildly.

I am sitting on the bed, doing nothing, and you're too worked up to notice how odd that is.

"Who?" Because there is no other reply.

"He accused me of plagiarizing!" You storm around my room, and if your eyes were focused and you didn't have a hurt throat you'd see your tennis racket sticking out from under my bed.

"Ansel Carter?"

"Yes, Ansel Carter! My English teacher? And you know how? Not because he's comparing my essay on Poe to some other text. Oh no. He accused me of plagiarizing because he said it was too sophisticated for me to have written it!"

"But—you're smart. Everyone knows you're smart."

"He doesn't think so. He thinks I'm a math head who can't write. Basically, he's profiling me!" you say, crying with rage.

"He has to prove it. And he can't, right?"

"Of course he can prove it. All he has to do is find the text I lifted it from."

"Wait. What?"

"I said he just has to google it. It's a matter of time."

"You're saying—wait. You're saying you did plagiarize?"

"I was rushed. I'm so angry at myself, I want, I want—" You hold clumps of hair and stare into my mirror, like you might rip your hair out, or maybe rip your own head off.

"This is the kind of thing you get flagged for," you rage on. "This is the kind of thing you get expelled for. This is the kind of thing you don't get into college for."

You drop your hair and lunge around the room, herky-jerky, muttering, "Stupid stupid stupid." You're scaring the crap out of me, and if I was hoping for a distraction from the mess I left in your father's desk drawer and the bag of loot sticking halfway out from under my bed, then I got it.

I grab your shoulders and sink you down onto the bed. "It's okay. Don't be hard on yourself. You're under so much pressure." I search for the right words, something between a sitcom mom and the phrases printed on the Lululemon bags in the pantry. "Everyone makes bad choices. Humans are flawed. You're human."

You look up, biting your lip gently.

"Deep breaths," I say.

You exhale long and hard. Finally, you say, "I guess everyone is flawed in some way, right?"

"Absolutely definitely yes." It comes out fast, too fast, Jo. Creepy. Pull back. "And on the upside, you're interesting. And incredibly fun. And a generous friend. These things count for something."

You drop back onto my bed and I do the same beside you. Our heads are close, and your hair falls across my bare arm. It must feel good to have hair like that, brushing against your own arms, down your bare back, and against your cheeks, when you want to hide inside it. I lift a chunk of it and tickle your arm, and you laugh, and it's a little bit of music.

"There are flaws that are worse than mine." You say it like a fact. Or maybe a test.

"Of course there are."

"You believe that?"

"I do." This is the truth, and the truth causes you to snuggle against me.

"You know, after you left, I kept pictures of you in my room. I made myself look at them every day," you say.

Yes you did, you poor thing. I'm starting to understand why you are so messed up. "Wasn't that tough?" I say.

"That's the point," you say. "I was trying to feel something. But there was nothing."

"I get that," I say, and I don't, but whatever. "I mean, there's something weird about a person just vanishing. What are you supposed to feel?"

You laugh at the ceiling, deep and lusty. "You are empathy incarnate. You're like an exotic pet."

I don't know how to take that, but you feel so good next to me, better than anyone has felt, even Wolf, whose heat was comforting, where your heat is exciting. You roll onto your side and prop yourself on your elbow. "I didn't know how I felt about you being back. Now, I can't imagine you gone," she says.

I stare at the ceiling. How am I supposed to scramble down that fire escape now, when you are the closest thing to love I have? I can feel this very thing flashing across my face, and I am losing it, until you lean over and whisper in my ear.

"Just to be clear. I don't regret that I did something bad. I regret that I got caught. I'm so much better than that."

I snap my head to look at her, and we burst out laughing. Temple Lovecraft, you are dazzling. You grab my hands and play with them. "You make my life so much better. I wish there was something I could do for you."

"Your parents took me in. I would have been with foster parents, probably, living in some sketchy home with twelve other foster kids. You and your family are doing everything you can for me. What else is there?"

You make a short disgusted snort. "My parents don't do anything without getting something in return."

"Most people don't." It was a Jo thing to say, but you're on a roll and don't notice.

"You disappeared at a time when people still remembered the story about the little girl who got kidnapped from the resort while her parents ate dinner. Unfortunate timing for Henry and Clarissa. Now they get to sweep in and make it right, be the parents who take in the girl they wronged, now an orphan. It's like a freaking Dickens novel. It's amazing how far a little goodwill will take you in this tiny town."

"It was the right thing to do," I say lamely.

"I'm not complaining. Mom and Dad are easier to deal with because they're happy about the good buzz, for Dad's business, and for the useless things my mother does. She's back in standing with the Junior League; I bet you didn't know that."

"I did not." I picture Clarissa Lovecraft in a baseball uniform, though that cannot be right.

"And there are other things." You roll back over and run your finger behind my ear, and I freeze, because there are three earring holes in that lobe, faint marks, barely noticeable, a weak moment in Immokalee when I was bored with a pin and ice, and I'd be willing to bet Vivi did not have thrice-pierced ears.

"Other things like . . . ?"

"It's like we got to exhale when you came back."

I pretend your touch tickles and squirm, burying my ear and its telltale holes in my shoulder. "Because of years of worry." My voice cracks.

"Something like that."

You stay in my room through supper, faking cramps, and I go along with it though I'm starving and really needed one last good meal. Mr. and Mrs. Lovecraft leave for "date night" and we watch *Friends* reruns on Netflix (reruns I've never seen, because: shed!) on your phone until I can't keep my eyes open. Once I am sure you're asleep, curled up like a ball with your sharp bum sticking out, I slide out of the bed, pull the bag out from under it, and head for the window.

I reach for the window sash, and there is Wolf.

He signals for me to raise it. I shake my head hysterically, mute, dropping the bag to the floor and kicking a blanket over it.

"The Last One," he mouths. My mouth runs dry and I tell myself Wolf can be silent: silent is what he does best. I check your sleeping body, watch the rise and fall of your breath for three counts, before sliding the window open. I sign for Wolf to follow me out of the room, across the hall into yours, and he does this, at my heels, and I smell cold night air trapped in his clothes. I press the door to your bedroom shut with a soft *click*.

Wolf stalks the room. "So this is your new sister's room?"

I whisper hoarsely, "What do you want?"

"If this is her room, then why was she sleeping in your bed?" he says.

" 'The Last One.' You said, 'The Last One.' What do you know?" I say.

He looks at me, long and pained.

"Wolf!" I cry.

"I don't even know why I'm here." He tries to push past, but I step in front of him. Jo is leaving tonight, and Jo needs to know what she's up against out there.

"You're here because you know the Last One will betray me," I say. "Now where is he?"

Wolf draws his hand over his face. "Tell me why I should even tell you."

"So I can be ready."

"You can be ready at Tent City."

I take his face in my hands. "I'm safer here."

"You don't need this family. I could keep you safe."

My eyes fall to the photos of Vivi on the vanity. The changes Vivi has brought. A thriving charity. Social acceptance. Goodwill. Mr. and Mrs. Lovecraft might know I'm not Vivienne Weir, but they don't care.

"Vivienne Weir is the only one who can keep me safe."

"A dead girl?" he says.

"A missing girl," I say, dropping his face and turning over his arms to check for new burns, and there they are, the puckers pink and fresh.

"I won't put you in danger," he murmurs, pulling his arms down and wrapping them around my waist. He presses against me, and what kind of mind-erasing place is this house that I've forgotten how perfectly Wolf and I fit together?

I finally understand his lie. "You're not here because the Last One has come. You wanted to be together one more time."

He covers my mouth with his before I can speak again, and I ache, an ache I hadn't known was there but that had been building for days, and all night, on the bed with you, and I drop my head back to let him kiss my throat, thinking about your mouth. The door creaks open. I spin around and stagger away from Wolf. You stand in the doorway, roused from sleep, your hair mashed up on one side. Your eyes are glazed, and you shut the door behind you quietly, and when you turn, your eyes have sharpened.

Words rush to my tongue. Your unkind smile stops me cold.

"Tell me, Vivi. How did you manage to make a friend when you never leave the house?" you say.

"He's not a friend."

You raise a finger. "Aha! So, he's a burglar. Bum who wandered off the street? Home invader?"

"I'm leaving," Wolf says, heading for the door.

You step in front of him. "Oh no, friend. You'll leave when I say it's time. Otherwise, I'll have to call Slade. And as Vivi knows, Slade needs things to do around here. After all, his only job is to protect his employers from their own daughter. When they're asleep in their beds, and can't protect themselves. Imagine what it's like to be afraid of your own child?"

You take Wolf's hand and my hand playfully and drag us to your bed, tossing us to the mattress like rag dolls while you lord over. "But it appears I'm not the one they have to worry about!"

"Temple . . . ," I start.

"Time for introductions!" you sing.

Wolf stands and you push him back down. He would never push a girl. Somehow you know this and use it.

"Sooo," you say, sarcastic-chipper. "How do we know each other?"

Wolf starts to speak, and I run over his words. "We met while I was missing. He—he was kept. In the shed."

Your eyes shine. "In the shed? Really? So the evil boogey-man liked little boys, too?"

I nod, flustered.

"Thank goodness you had each other!" You sway with your words. "And from the looks of it, you got to know each other pretty well. Missed each other, even. Had to make up for lost time. Tell me your name, Victim Number Two."

Wolf looks to me anxiously. I look only at you.

"They call me Wolf," he says.

"You're beautiful, Wolf. Look at you, though! You're perfect. That face. If I didn't know your . . . situation, I'd say you were a hot, brooding English actor. Your life hasn't made your face hard. Yet. Not so much for Vivi here. Life hasn't been so kind to her."

I shift in my spot on the mattress. Where are you going with this?

"You see how rough her hands are?" You grab my wrists and yank me off the bed and force my hands under Wolf's nose. "And the white ridges in her fingernails? The gauntness to her cheeks: okay, I guess that's gone away. We've been feeding her pretty well here."

I yank my hands back and plead, "Your parents will be home any second. Wolf has to go."

"Back to Tent City?" you say.

"What did you say?" I say it slowly. This is the end, oh yes it is.

"I've known you're not Vivi since the moment we met. You're a stranger to this family. Admittedly, the perfect stranger."

Wolf stands. "We're both out of here." He walks toward the door, and this time you don't stop him. He looks to me, frozen in place.

"You've known?" I whisper, falling back down on the bed.

"Of course I've known. And it doesn't matter. None of it matters." You lean to stroke my cheek. "I'll give you anything you want if you stay. What do you want most in this world, Vivi?"

"Jo, now. Let's go," Wolf begs.

"Love? I'll love you," you say.

"Jo," Wolf says.

"Security? You have it here. You're safe with us. You aren't safe on the streets," you say.

"Temple," I whisper, burying my face in my hands.

"Money? Comfort? We can give you all of it," you say.

"That's not it. I don't . . ." I can't say *Momma*, because Momma is dead, and she may have loved me but she was not good for me. I can't say *family*, because the truth is, I would be happy with just you.

What do I want?

"Jolene!" Wolf cries. "This is the last time I'll ask you. Are you coming?"

"I see." Your smile spreads. "I'm already giving you what you need, aren't I?"

Your eyes are pools and I see my tiny self inside them. I fit inside you and I bet you fit inside me. There is no more need for Vivi. I can be myself with you now, and this is not nothing.

Wolf roils with hate and pain. I know what he is going home to do, and there is nothing I can do about it and I am the cause.

"Tell him to go, Vivi," you say.

"Jo!" Wolf says: a warning.

"Tell him!" you say.

I rise and go to Wolf, kissing him gently on the sharp jut

of his cheek. "Please go," I whisper into his neck. He pours a long look on me that I turn my back on, and I can feel it there, burning a hole, and my eyes fill with tears. We are still and silent, the three of us, but for my hitching sounds as I try not to cry. Wolf and I might see each other again, when we are older and freer and I don't need what I need. I flash on our moments together, against each other's skin, in the hot tent and the cold tent and under the stars, and I wonder if I ever really loved Wolf, or just absorbed his beauty while I could, the way everyone who uses Wolf does. Finally, the door closes, and I hear the distant scrape of a window being raised and the jangle of the shaking fire escape.

"For the record," you say, coming closer, "we never buttered the cat."

I steel myself and raise my eyes. "How did you know I wasn't Vivi?"

"Because I know what happened to the real Vivi. Would you like me to tell you?"

"Yes."

PART II
TEMPLE

"*B*oston, May 2010. Two girls, both nine. The streets are filled with wine-buzzed lovers. Packs of graduates having one last night out before everyone scatters. Expensive cars driven by European students heading to Newbury Street for drinks before going to the clubs. In her room, the mother sprays perfume that drifts in front of the cold fireplace where the girls sit in pajamas, bowl of popcorn at their feet, mollifying Disney show already on. It is a room the parents make excuses for: plastic covers a square in the wall, an unsightly hole made by their contractor. The parents are young and their lives are exciting. A new deal has been inked, a deal that means enough money to commence their plan of buying the empty brownstone for sale next door, gutting it and expanding. They want to celebrate. They want to forget for a night that their nine-year-old daughter tries to control them by pitching a fit every time they leave her with a sitter. Fits that they joke with their friends about, leaving out the scratches and the bruises and the mortal threats.

"The friend keeps the girl happy. She is the daughter of European friends on the same block, quality people who do not parent like hovering aircraft the way American parents do. The girl is usually content with this friend: a meek, compliant girl who lives happily in the other girl's shadow. The parents are optimistic. All week the sleepover was the carrot for good behavior. Sleepovers are supposed to be fun, not occasions for hysterics.

"The father's heavy footsteps, oily fingerprints on his pants from the girl clinging to his legs, desperate for him to stay. Swears from the father, soothing words from the mother, a change of pants. She is nine, for goodness' sake. The friend is used to the girl's outbursts, but she is still embarrassed, and pretends to be deeply interested in the Disney show, her nose nearly touching the TV. The girl grows quiet, a slow, controlled burn. The mother takes away the popcorn: choking hazard. Phone numbers are left, promises are made to return early. They will be just one door over, visible from the window of Daddy's office. They will request a seat on the patio, and the girls can wave to them from the window.

"Doors are locked from the outside. Behind the door, the parents exchange sighs of relief and hold hands. It will be fine. She cannot control their lives. They are good parents. They're no farther away than if they were sitting on their own front steps and the girls were inside. Inside, the friend wants to play with their American Girl dolls, hers brought for the occasion, a little blond doppelgänger with hard cheeks. The girl has no interest. The girl walks to the father's darkened office and stares out at the patio, at her parents being seated by a hostess, at her parents looking into each other's eyes, and never once looking up and waving at the window, like they'd promised. The girl waits and waits and waits. The friend calls her to come, this is no fun, they can watch any show she wants. There is no specialness in this, of course, since the girl is always in charge of what they watch. The parents clink their drinks and smile at each other and touch hands, and the girl watches and grows cold. Inside her, the tiny flame that has burned dimmer and dimmer each passing year finally snuffs out. She turns away and glides into the kitchen on pale feet, big for a girl of nine. She will be tall.

"The girl turns the big old stove to four twenty-five. For good measure, she twists the numbered knobs on the front too, which go click-click-click. Nothing happens except a smell the girl associates with her mother cooking, so she thinks that must be right. From a deep drawer, she takes out a hand mixer, a shiny bowl, a cake pan, and a spatula. From the pantry, she takes out cake mix, and from the refrigerator, eggs and butter.

"She waits. A minute, two. Lets the darkness within rise and meet her. From the living room, the TV roars canned laughter.

" 'I want to bake,' she calls to the friend. The friend jumps up with a cheer.

"The girl reads the box of cake mix. 'It says we need oil. Can you get it from the top shelf?'

"The friend is small and stands on her toes to reach. The girl holds the hand mixer by its skinny neck and swings it like a bottle. The crack against the back of the friend's head is swift and pleasing. The friend staggers, stunned, her eyes unfocused, inexplicably smiling. She says the girl's name like a question. The oven dings. The girl walks wide of the staggering friend, who is reaching for her, and opens the oven door with a squeal. The friend teeters; her back is small. The girl grasps the back of the friend's pajamas and shoves her headfirst into the oven, knocking the door partly closed with her knee. Holds her there. The friend barely struggles. The girl doesn't know if she's doing it right, but the smell of gas is strong and the friend stops struggling after a minute. Slowly, the girl drags the friend from the oven (so light! Filled with sawdust, this friend) and lays her on the floor back in the parlor in front of the TV. The girl considers the open wall; peels back the plastic. It is a lovely nook, a place the girl would like to hide in, if she needed to. Folding the friend makes her fit. The girl tapes the plastic back in place. Behind, the friend is a rosy blur.

"The girl follows the slug trail of blood back to the kitchen. She is getting a dull headache. Holding her head, she closes the oven door and reaches for the oil. Measures the oil, cracks the eggs, pours the powdery mix into the bowl. She cleans the friend's blood off the base of the hand mixer with a paper towel and mixes the cake, a soft whir over the noise of the Disney show. She moves the bowl to a different counter so she can watch the show at the same time. When the characters do something silly, she laughs, even though it is a show she's already seen. When the mix is poured and the cake is in the oven, she returns to the window, leaving the mess on the counter, because she is nine. Her parents have ordered dessert, and it has arrived, and they are sharing the small cup of crème brûlée. This is the girl's favorite dessert, and she can taste the caramelized sugar in her mouth. They must hate her, to do this to her. To leave her alone with the memory of burnt sugar in a house smelling of gas and chocolate and blood.

"The girl remembers the cake. She turns on the oven light and peers inside, but it tells her nothing. She tries taking the cake out, but because she is nine, she forgets oven mitts and burns her palms, dropping the cake upside down on the floor. She runs her hands under cold water until they turn numb, and this is how they find her."

The only sound is my ragged breathing as it slows to nothing. Temple gazes at her open hands, tilting them, as if they still shine with burns, and continues:

"The girl shows them her hands, but they ignore her. Shouts about the gas, running to throw open windows that will be barred in the months ahead. The mother hammers at her cell phone but it is dead and she blames this on the husband. At the same time, they see the cake on the floor. They want to know where the friend is. The girl points to the parlor. The father stares at the girl for a moment, recognizing that the light in her has gone out, while the mother rushes to the parlor yelling for the friend. The mother grows quiet. The father comes toward the girl. The mother calls the father's name, unsure, trembling. The girl's hands hurt. She holds them out for him to see. Her eyes are dry. The father rips his eyes away from the girl and joins the mother in the parlor. The girl twists the faucet back on and sticks her hands underneath.

"Above the gush of water, the sound of plastic ripped from plaster.

"The screams come and come and then stop, a hand over a mouth. Open windows, dining people. The danger of it. There will be no time for screams.

"Windows are shut. Hammering, the dragging and placing of heavy furniture. The smell of wooden floor cleaner. A building permit sticker repositioned prominently in the window. The girl's hands are finally bandaged and she is put to bed. Nerves are soothed and phone calls are made.

"The girl smiles, listening to her parents speak to the police officers below. This time, she is sure they will not leave her again."

. . . . .

You kick your feet and jump off the bureau, pulling the shirt you're wearing over your head, hair spilling over your back. Fully aware of your nakedness, as you dig too long for a big T-shirt to pull on. When you rise, you flip your hair back to perfect and sigh.

"Now it's time for you to tell me a story," you say.

"You know my story. Your father hired a private investigator and he pulled everything on my life in Florida." If you have a shred of feeling for me in your heart, this is the time for me to find it and use it. "You know exactly how much my life sucked."

"I understand completely. On her own, Jolene Chastain has nothing. She needs food. Clothes. A place to live. A phone. A computer. An education. She got these things, plus something she didn't know she wanted until she had it."

I say nothing.

"And what would that thing be?" you tease. "C'mon, say it."

"Temple . . . ," I say softly.

"That's right! Me! Your soul mate." You grab my hand and drag me into the bed. My heart races. We're head to head again, this time, in your bed, and you aren't letting me go anywhere. "Now I want that story."

We lie for a while. You are patient when you know you're going to get something. Every time I blink, I see Vivi reaching high on her tiptoes, a smack to the back of her head, blinding pain, starfish hands reaching out for a mother who isn't there.

"Vivi? The story."

I swallow thickly. "I always knew she would die."

"The year, please."

"What?"

"When did she die?"

"You already know this. You know everything."

"Tell the story properly, please."

I exhale hard. "It was 2016 when she died."

"When she died, or when she was killed?"

"You know the answer to that."

"That's an important distinction, wouldn't you say? Isn't that the point of the whole story, Jolene Chastain?"

You wrap your arm around mine and snuggle against my shoulder. What have I gotten myself into? The sensation of falling, into the bed, through the bed and through two floors, through the room below where the real Vivi's bones are encased in a wall, past her bones and through the earth, to its molten core, where you and I will burn together. Wolf couldn't have saved me from the streets, or even the Last One, but he could have saved me from you.

Wolf is gone, and I am a fool.

"It was 2016 when my momma's last boyfriend killed her," I say. "My life was about keeping her alive. She had my love, and still she thought she should die. Every drug. Every scheme. Every boyfriend was laced through with danger. But this story is about the one thing that finally did kill her. He had a name, but I'm not gonna use it, because he doesn't deserve a name. I call him the Last One.

"In the end, I believe Momma wanted to live. Otherwise she wouldn't have tried to escape. While she didn't care about her own life, she cared about mine. When she started to realize that the Last One would take mine, too, that made her ready to run. But he cut her down.

"The weekend before I left, we made a good score. He wanted to celebrate. She never saw him touch me until that night.

"You're wondering why I didn't tell her. It would have made her run with me sooner.

"But it wasn't like that. We needed enough money to get away first, and besides, she wasn't in any shape to leave. She was still getting clean off meth, tapering her doses, and a mess so much of the time. Sleeping, depressed. He took advantage of her sleeping to come to me, and it was everything I could do not to kill. I kept a knife under my pillow so I knew it was there, and when he was on me, I'd fantasize about plunging it through the hard gristle of him, then a pillow of blood as it pierced the heart, a whoosh. I'd slip out from underneath his still body and walk away, like

Carrie White, covered in his blood, strong and straight-backed and avenged.

"But killing boyfriends would've given us another problem.

"So I sent myself to another place to get through it. I focused on weaning Momma from using every day to twice a week, from a quarter gram to an eighth of a gram, and pretty soon she'd be clear. The Last One didn't care: he was glad for it. Thought she was useless high. But she took so long to come out of it, ate and slept so much it pissed him off, and pretty soon he'd carved Momma out of his scams so it was him and me, operating as a team, or what he thought was a team, since my eyes were only on the money.

"Arrangements were made online. I'd wait, alone, watching the TV but really listening to the sound of the highway outside—there was always a highway right outside—behind the heavy curtains. The sound of cars rushing by was the sound of escape. A flash of headlights through the curtains, a careful knock on the door. I always had to be something different, a call I had to make on the spot. If the mark had a squirrelly look to him, it meant that this was the first time he had done something like this, and he needed proof that I knew what I was doing. The ones that asked my age straightaway wanted a young girl, so I'd tell him I was nine, but an early bloomer—there was something magical about single digits. They were the same ones who wanted to get down to business right away, and were the hardest to stall. They were the reason I had a code phrase—'Would you like to take a shower first?'—that meant Mad Daddy needed to burst into the room that very second.

"Mad Daddy was part of the act, of course. The Last One would bust in hollering, claiming my addict mom had set the whole thing up and he knew nothing about it. Naturally, pictures would be taken. Threats made. Money handed over.

"Sometimes I got mine. I knew the Last One liked to watch from next door on a video camera he set up, so I did obnoxious things to the camera behind the mark's back. Flipping the Last One off, for example. He knew there was danger for me, being alone too long. Not from the mark, who would look around the room like he didn't know how he got there and then grow sad. These were the ones that cried hardest and paid fastest. The one with a glint in his eye when he saw no adult had bothered to attend the 'transaction'—these were the ones to fear. They saw a girl alone and they thought, *jackpot*.

"But the kind of mark didn't matter to the Last One. He only had to swoop into the room and cash in on our double payment: first, the arrangement fee collected online, second, the extortion fee, which could go on forever, since we had the mark's personal info. A payment plan for sin, he called it. Anyway. This one time toward the end, we made a killing, because the mark was what they call a 'public figure,' with a lot to lose and deep pockets. A guy with pale hair and a wife and seven kids. He was a politician for one of those states where the people all call themselves Christian but have lots of wives and whatever. Point is, the guy had to pay whatever we asked for or kill himself out of shame, which he did anyway one year later. The Last One got so drunk celebrating that night that he stumbled in and forgot Momma was in the bed next to us. Making noise about doing to me what the marks never got to, and for that he was The Man. I remember laying there thinking about a new fantasy, the scene in one of those *Silence of the Lambs* movies, not the first one, but maybe the second or third, where they train the pigs to eat the bad guy's face off, and how perfect a fate that would be for him, and wondering where you'd get such pigs.

"That's when Momma woke up.

"I saw her first, her eyes wide in the stripe of parking

lot light coming through the parted drapes. She blinked and blinked and then sat straight up in her bed, and I flinched underneath him, because I knew the jolt must have hurt her head. She screamed, grabbed the back of his shirt, and tore him off me, and he swore like I've never heard anyone swear, staggering around the tiny room, banging into a desk and knocking over a lamp, and I scrambled up and pulled Momma away, because I knew that he would kill her. He was drunk, really drunk, and couldn't get his balance, and when Momma screamed for me to get into the bathroom and lock myself in, I did.

"He hurt her bad that night, though by some miracle of God he passed out before he killed her. We moved on to a new hotel, and the scams ran the same. But after that night, a switch flipped inside the Last One. He stopped touching me. He got panicky, using the money to buy us dumb presents like a big microwave for the hotel room and a bracelet for Momma with little glass beads, each one with some special meaning. She took it and thanked him but didn't mean it, and once he left, I watched her whip it against the bathroom sink until each bead had starburst cracks. On my birthday, he brought home a cheesecake from a factory that made only cheesecakes, any kind you could think of, and my cake was called Death by Chocolate and I kept thinking *Death by Flesh-Eating Pigs*. Momma stopped using altogether, though she didn't tell him. She pretended to sleep all the time still, but mostly, she watched. She skimmed money off our grocery allowance, and that money went inside the cookie tin. It was unsaid between us, what she was doing, because she wanted to keep me safe, but I knew. It wasn't easy. He watched her closer than ever. It wasn't her that was so valuable to him, of course: it was me. The hotel scam brought in more money than any scam before, and he'd learned that we could run it without her. I guess that's why, when he found the hidden money, and the name of the shelter we were leaving for that same night, he beat her to death.

"After Momma was gone, there was a buzzing around me, black insects, I imagined, that crusted my eyes and nose, a rot that could take me out of this world if I let it. I had to act fast. Momma had spent most of her life trying to die, but I had spent most of mine trying to live. I took that whorl of black-winged rage and pain and sucked it inside, let it fill up my chest and lungs. My back got straighter, my eyes clearer, my mind sharper with their humming inside me, and I controlled that rage, converted it into something powerful. It led me to my escape.

"The last time he touched me was six weeks before he

killed Momma: enough time to convince him I needed to buy a pregnancy test.

"The thing about the Last One is, he's a con. A con is always thinking about their next move, the longer term, three steps ahead, when they should be thinking about the here and now. Instead of thinking, 'I'm giving Jolene a chance to escape,' the Last One was thinking about where he would dump my body if that stick showed two pink lines. Or, if there was one pink line, how this was a wake-up call to get me birth control, and where was the closest free clinic? And also, since Patty was out of the picture now, wasn't it time to get back to our old ways? He fixed on these things as I slipped the keys out of his pocket. He fixed on these things as he asked the gas station attendant for the Early Result pregnancy test. He fixed on these things as I slid into my seat on a Greyhound Bus bound for Boston with half the money from that last scam, and the driver pulled the door closed."

"You became Vivi to hide," you murmur, breathing deeply.

"Yes." *No. I became Vivi to have a family. To have you. But I cannot say these things because you'll see me as weak, and to be weak around you is the most dangerous of all.*

"The insects—that feeling. It's still there?"

"Yes."

"In your chest and lungs and—"

"I said yes," I snap.

You smile. "Then you'll need to control it."

"I can control it. Most girls would have crumbled. I let it lift me. It's what drove me to escape."

"It will also destroy you if you don't learn how to use it."

I roll to face you. "How do you know this?"

"I have it inside me, too." You wet your lips. "And I can teach you to use it."

We move to my room and climb out the window left open by Wolf, you first, to the roof. I didn't know you could get to the roof from the fire escape; I only considered it as a way down. It's windy on the tarred roof, but you bring the plaid blanket that you gave me a few long weeks ago, when you first gave me your warmth, and you have climbed up here before. We wrap ourselves in it and lie on our backs, your leg slung over mine, owning me. The sky is full with city light, and dark clouds pass, close and fast.

"I'm going to go quickly. If you don't get it, I'm not going to explain it to you," you say, and I am not patient with fools, either.

"That feeling is your power. That's what lifted you out of that crappy hotel room away from your dead mother's boyfriend when most girls would have clung to him because it was all they knew. That's what drove you out of Tent City and into our home. And when they come for you—the doubters and the cops and whoever else figures out you aren't Vivi, and they will—you need to use that power to stand your ground. Pretending you're Vivi isn't enough. You need to get rid of them. That's where your rage takes over."

I sit up on one elbow. "Get rid of them?"

"You should be prepared to. Selectively eliminating threats is completely realistic. But you have to practice. Use your rage when it isn't necessary. The most effective predators attack prey without an immediate need or use for it. It's called surplus killing. Think of wolves killing a whole henhouse of hens and eating just one. They're not killing for the fun of it. They're honing their reflexes, their skills. You need to exercise your rage, or it will get dull. I do this myself, and I can help you do it, too."

I think of fencing. You're talking about fencing, I'm sure of it.

"That said, you have to hide it. Blunt the sharp edges. When a victim shows rage, it's called admirable. In a predator, rage is a lack of humanity. It scares people. Shape yourself so no one can see it."

"I guess."

"You need to be prepared. Once your rage takes over, there is no grasp of reality or balance until it's exhausted. You'll find yourself looking down at what you've done, and the shock will creep in. Resist. You need to get your head together fast to figure out how to get away with it."

I think you are telling me to kill people who get in my way of being Vivi. You've said it before: we are natural-born killers. But I'm going to pretend you aren't, because we are here under this big sky and you are warm and I have nowhere else to go.

I shiver underneath the blanket. You draw me nearer.

"You and me: we're like sticks. Apart we were easily broken, but together we're strong." You bend and kiss my head. "Never leave me."

We lie like this against each other. I watch my breath in clouds over my face. After a while, you slip from under the blanket and start the climb down.

I sit up. "Where are you going?"

"To bed. It's a school night."

My world is upside down and you are thinking about

getting sleep for your classes tomorrow. You stop on the ladder before your head disappears.

"Oh, also: my parents were right. You should totally do the *Today Show*."

. . . . .

Three days later the *Today Show* sends a limo to pick up Mr. and Mrs. Lovecraft and me at an ungodly hour. It's four hours and twenty minutes of a near-silent ride, where everyone is absorbed in their own electronics and reading materials. I try to ask Mrs. Lovecraft what I am expected to do and say, but she insists I need only tell the truth: we are a family, I am doing well, and everything is better.

It would have been better if you were here.

"Do you think maybe this could backfire? Like, it could make the reporters more interested?" I sound so stupid. Straddling the line between being innocent Vivi and knowing they know I am Jo means everything I say comes out sounding like a backward woman-child.

Mrs. Lovecraft takes off the glasses she wears to read. "Are you having second thoughts?"

"No. I get why this is good. Once the world knows I

don't remember anything, the police can't push," I say, puppet that I am.

"That's exactly right. As far as the press goes, never doubt that we can protect you." She pats my knee. "We've been through this before. We will always be able to protect you."

As we drive deeper into New York, towers crowd the sun and everything turns gray. I've never seen New York, but I say nothing of this. When Mr. Lovecraft says, "There's Lady Liberty!" I bob my head to see. Thirty Rock, as Mr. Lovecraft calls it, is like Quincy Market on steroids, with fountains and distracted tourists. How easy it would be to pickpocket, and I banish the thought, for that is not the right mind-set for today. I want to stop and see the fountain and the golden statue, but the Lovecrafts are serious, and this is not a time to be a goofy tourist. We arrive in a lobby where the air smells pumped in and ride a fancy elevator, exiting into another lobby with huge posters of the show's hosts. The receptionist asks our names and tells us to go directly to the greenroom, which is not green but orange, with a feast of pastries that has me drooling. From here you can watch the show in real time on one of the flat-screen TVs, and I don't, because it freaks me out. The Lovecrafts don't, either. A quick-talking woman rescues us from our nerves. She identifies herself as our producer, treating me like a piece of china, which is good, because it helps me get back into character. What she doesn't do is tell us what they're going to ask. We're supposed to go on at 8:35, and we're waiting for a fourth person. The producer sighs when at 8:02, Harvey Silver strides in, pink stripes down his gray suit, legs and arms scissoring like a grasshopper. He shakes Mr. Lovecraft's hand and kisses Mrs. Lovecraft on the cheek. I am starting to feel like an afterthought, as in I wouldn't be surprised if they didn't notice if I stayed in the greenroom, and this is good, too, actually. Harvey asks where you are, to "complete the family picture," and the only words I hear are "unpredictable," and he nods knowingly, and I am not surprised.

We are hustled into Hair and Makeup, capital *H* and capital *M*, and they apply makeup like mad to everybody, including Harvey and Mr. Lovecraft. I sneak a glance at Mrs. Lovecraft in the chair beside me and mirror her stillness, the way she raises her eyes when they sweep and spackle. When Momma wore makeup, it looked like her only better, but the stuff they are putting on Mrs. Lovecraft makes her look like a clown, and I assume clown colors look good on TV. Most people change their clothes, but no one gave us that memo, and the woman in charge of my hair frowns at my wrinkled skirt, and she should cut me some slack since we just drove four hours. Suddenly I am in my underwear and shoes behind a curtain in the corner of Hair and Makeup and a hungover intern is steaming my skirt. When I step into it, it burns my bare thighs.

While I was standing in my underwear, the others disappeared. The intern rushes me to the studio where a big digital clock reads 8:12. We are to be interviewed by the prettiest woman I have ever seen. Natalie is tiny, with sucked-in pockets underneath her cheekbones and a dress the color of bubble gum. Her arms are impossibly tight in cap sleeves, and I can't stop staring at them. She sits in the chair opposite us and introduces herself, shaking our hands. She oozes health and energy and Mr. Lovecraft is oozing admiration, and I am vaguely irritated. When she takes my hand I stare at hers, a perfect little shell, with perfect fingernails edged with little white moons. She pulls away with a pretty frown.

And it is 8:35 and we are on. They are on; I am silent. I don't need to speak, because they are playing a montage of my life—Vivi's life—along with pictures of her chum parents, and Mrs. Lovecraft is tearing up. Apparently they wanted to do a "walking and talking shot" of me and Natalie, but there wasn't enough time to tape it, and this is good because I don't love the idea of America having a nice long chance to compare images of Jolene Chastain with images of Vivienne Weir. Natalie and Harvey are doing most of the talking, and I can see us on the monitors behind the cameras, and when Natalie asks each of us a question, the camera focuses on that person. Now Natalie is asking Mrs. Lovecraft what our "reunion" was like, and reunions make me think of big happy families and long picnic tables and matching shirts. The camera zooms in on Mrs. Lovecraft, and she is fiddling with her hands in her lap. Above the waist and on camera, she is perfectly still and composed, and I am weirdly proud.

"Seeing Vivi again, healthy and strong, was the second happiest moment of my life. The first was giving birth to my own daughter," Mrs. Lovecraft says.

This is Natalie's segue into that night. She recounts the hours while Vivi went missing, and the Lovecrafts reach for each other's hands, when shouldn't they be reaching for mine? Then Natalie mentions the unspoken: the flak the Lovecrafts got afterward, as careless parents. And then she's on to the Weirs' plane crash, and the fact of my orphaning, and don't you feel bad for me, people? Natalie is brilliant. Natalie is a star. Natalie deserves her fat paycheck. Because without having to defend or deny, we are back to sympathy and admiration for the Lovecrafts, and it is my turn to say something.

I know this because she says, "I want to give Vivienne a chance to say something."

I swallow at America.

"First, please accept our condolences on the loss of your parents. After all this time, do you feel like you are finally home?" asks Natalie.

I look directly into the camera trained on my face. Vivi's crinkle-nosed smile is not an option: I will look deranged. I go for something straddling the line between shy and sad. "Um. I miss my parents, of course. In a way, I'm lucky, I think, not to remember anything about the last seven years. Being found—it's kind of like a rebirth. A second chance at my life."

This was the right thing to say. You can feel hearts softening around the studio, murmurs of agreement: yes, it is her second chance, yes, it is a rebirth, let's forget she probably got abducted and doesn't remember anything about the last seven years, that's a downer, all is well, what a wonderful world!

Natalie wishes us every good thing, and me especially,

and it is done, over, and it was *so fast* and now the world knows me as Vivi. Mr. Lovecraft lingers, getting the most out of his time with Natalie, who is used to men and wants to get away from him.

By 8:55 we are back in the limo, which apparently kept circling around the block to avoid cops and tickets. I have whiplash from the speed at which this thing happened. By two thirty, we're pulling up in front of 999 Common-wealth Avenue.

Mrs. Lovecraft leans over to me. "Just like I said. We nipped it in the bud with this one interview. We don't—you don't—owe them anything else."

Mr. Lovecraft smiles at me, but it's more like a grimace. "One and done."

I nod. They can't imagine how much I would like this to be over with. Every time my face shows up on the screen, it's a chance for someone to pop out of the woodwork and claim I'm not Vivi.

A pack of reporters stands at the curb. There is a fester-ing quality about them, like maggots, tight-packed, jostling for the same space.

The limo driver leans over the seat. "Good luck getting into your own house."

His breath smells of stale coffee and I shoot him a dirty look.

"We're never getting out of the car!" Mrs. Lovecraft cries, her voice stippled with fear.

Mr. Lovecraft pats his pocket for his phone, finds it and calls Slade, cursing softly when he doesn't answer.

"Try him again," Mrs. Lovecraft urges.

Mr. Lovecraft calls again.

We stare at one another for a second, two. Mrs. Lovecraft grips my leg and gasps, "The car is spinning."

"The car is parked," I say, gently peeling her off my thigh. Her hand trembles, and I notice her hair is damp at the temples.

"Stay with us, Clarissa," Mr. Lovecraft says, hammering at his phone again. "Wake up, Slade. Wake up," he whispers.

"What's wrong with her?" I ask Mr. Lovecraft.

"She's having a panic attack. Just hang on, honey. Slade will clear a path for us in a minute and we'll be safe inside. You have to hang on," he says, phone jammed to his ear to hear over the growing hum outside the car.

"This is worse than I thought it would be," she murmurs into her hands, peeking through her fingers at the crowd. "So much worse."

"I don't mean to be rude, but I need to get to my next call," the driver calls over the seat.

"Our security man will be here any second," Mr. Lovecraft says.

"Hope you're not paying him much," the driver replies.

"Look!" Mrs. Lovecraft says, pointing out the window over her husband's shoulder.

"Finally!" Mr. Lovecraft hisses.

Slade charges down the stairs, puffing his chest and wearing a Bluetooth earpiece that might be a prop. His hair is mashed up in the back and he is blinking away sleep, and he might be late but he is *on*, shoving reporters aside like a superhero. He opens the limo door with one hand and makes way with his other massive arm. As we climb from the limo, the reporters are on us, on me, and I get shoved around. It is everything I can do not to beat down one of these very small, very made-up reporters, men included, though I, too, have lips stained TV-burgundy.

Mr. Lovecraft turns to the crowd.

"If you want a comment, you have to be quiet!" Mr. Lovecraft is cupped-hands-around-the-mouth yelling, and they listen, because he is a powerful man, and also, he must look good on TV. A reporter with cleavage shoves a mic in front of his mouth, and five mics follow. Mrs. Lovecraft pinches her neck, barely able to stand. I want to pull her inside, get her some water and a couch to lie on, but Mr. Lovecraft draws me between them. There is no room for you, even if you were here, on the steps, and am I their new daughter?

Mr. Lovecraft booms, "Today my wife Clarissa and I shared with the world the news of the miraculous return of Vivienne Weir, who disappeared seven years ago from this very town house. We are honored, humbled, and blessed to have been given custodial rights to Vivienne by her tragically deceased parents, our dear friends, Travis and Marie Weir, who specified this wish in their wills. As we welcome Vivi into our home with open arms, it is our sincere belief that we have been given another chance to make things right, and we hope that you will respect our desire for privacy at this time."

Cameras flash and video rolls and I gaze at the jawline of this man who says beautiful, unrehearsed things. I believe every word. Questions nail us from every side, and I think of battle scenes with flaming arrows shooting over our heads.

"Is it true she remembers nothing of the last seven years?"

"Is it confirmed that Vivienne was actually abducted?"

"Has Vivienne been diagnosed with a traumatic brain injury?"

"Are there plans to adopt Vivienne?"

"What about your daughter, Temple? How is she taking the news?"

Mr. Lovecraft puts his arms around us and draws us up the stairs of the town house. We keep our heads down. I count the steps: six, five, four, three, two . . .

"Henry Lovecraft!" A man's voice soars over the crowd. I recognize the direction: it was a small man hanging out in the back, leaning against a gaslight lamp, with no camera, just a *Boston Globe* press badge. "Is it true that your firm has lost six of its ten major contracts with the city since Vivienne Weir's abduction? As a developer, does her miraculous return mean anything for your own commercial success?"

Mr. Lovecraft halts. He is pissed. I am pissed. I don't fully understand it, but I do get that it's a rude question and someone should crack the little troll across the mouth.

Mrs. Lovecraft's thin voice wavers. "Don't respond, Henry. You're better than that."

He turns, leading with his chin, and the look in his eye scares me. I spin to face the cameras and raise my palms. The reporters go silent, and the only sounds are the roar of cars down Commonwealth Avenue and the clacks of cameras.

"I am Vivienne Weir," I call out. "And this is my family now. I consider myself the luckiest girl in the world."

I feel Mr. Lovecraft's anger drain out of him. He pulls me close to his leg with one hand and presses his heart with his fist. Mrs. Lovecraft leans against my shoulder and weeps. The reporters are swarming, regrouping, and we need to escape. Finally, Slade herds us through the front door with his massive hands, one unit, a mother, father, and daughter, impenetrable.

You stand on the other side of the door, and I am in your arms.

"You were perfect," you murmur into my hair. "I couldn't have done it better myself."

. . . . .

The Lovecrafts went out alone to celebrate this night, and for some reason you are shunning me, holed up in your room. I hear the Lovecrafts stumble in, laughing. They laugh like you, free and easy, and something in them has been rekindled lately. They stay up for an extra hour making love, and the noises wake up something inside me I wish would stay asleep, something I know is not useful to surviving here at 999 Commonwealth Avenue. When the house is silent, I creep downstairs to the parlor, which I am beginning to think of as the killing room. The darkness is more purple than black. I try to imagine this space seven years ago, a room less adult then and more for a little kid and her toys. Where a TV may have been. A huge antique floor mirror leans against the wall, and I use my back to hold it in place while I touch the wall behind, running my palm down to feel for seams and plastering. There, the faintest ridge, extending in the shape of a rectangle. The cutout is nearly identical in shape and size to the mirror, and a chill settles in the small of my back. I understand now why the Lovecrafts bought the brownstone next door but never expanded into it. Some walls ought to remain.

I place my cheek against the wall. I want to say I'm sorry, but I can't, because I'm not.

That night I dream of Momma. We're in the Dwiggins room, that marionette room in the library, and we are doing a new con, but my time is running out to learn it. Also, Momma has to be quiet explaining it to me, because we're not supposed to be in the Dwiggins room. I can't seem to wrap my brain around it, and there is something desperate about Momma; if I don't get this new con, something terrible is going to happen. But I can't think straight. It's complicated, this con, but I am older and I should be able to get it. Momma is frustrated, is trying to regress me, something she used to do when I couldn't get the right lifetime in my head, but it's like she's speaking a different language. Finally, Momma takes a key out of her ear, like a magician with a penny, and unlocks one of the cases.

"Don't!" I cry, because I know those marionettes are mean mothers and they're just waiting to get out from under that glass and chew our limbs off with their clickety-clackety mouths.

"I'm going to act it out for you," Momma says, pulling out two dolls.

And there I have to sit, watching Momma with seams across her face where the Last One smashed it in, holding two puppets high in the air, acting out the trick I am supposed to perform, but Momma isn't tall enough and the wooden feet and buckled legs keep dragging on the glass case. Footsteps and voices approach, along with the unmistakable yelling of guards, and dogs barking, and I keep trying to tell Momma we have to run, and it's the old panic again, the one I felt when I knew the Last One was going to kill her. But Momma ignores the noises, insisting I learn the con . . .

I sit up in my bed. Window, chair, nightstand. Moonlight on the fire escape, neon clock. My chest pounds and skitters dangerously. I think I am having a heart attack. I peel the sheets down and they stick to my sweaty legs, and I fight to free myself. Through my window I hear the demented yells of the last of the drunk college students heading toward Fenway. I swing my legs over the side of the bed and hoist myself across the hall to the bathroom, splashing cold water on my cheeks until they grow numb.

In the mirror, I see Momma's face, blank with fear.

. . . . .

Sunday morning is impossibly bright, and the Lovecrafts sleep in, probably hungover, and I am hungover on my nightmare. Confessing murder agrees with you, on the other hand. When I stumble downstairs you sit at the table already pouring milk, showered, fully dressed, hair glossy in a high ponytail. Slade lurks around the edges, drinking coffee behind his newspaper, hangdog like he got railed at yesterday for leaving us cowering in the limo. Mr. and

Mrs. Lovecraft stroll down the stairs, swatting each other with their bathrobe ties, giggling.

A glob of Honey Nut Cheerios gets stuck in my throat. I gulp milk and swallow hard.

You pour more cereal into your bowl. "So are you guys gonna tell Vivi the good news or make me wait some more?"

Mr. and Mrs. Lovecraft sweep into their seats. Mrs. Lovecraft pours coffee for herself and Mr. Lovecraft, and Slade looks increasingly uncomfortable, and they must have asked him to stay up.

"Mom?" you say, impatient.

"Yes, all right, Temple. Vivi, the news has to do with you. Actually, it's more than one thing. First, we've decided you should go to the Parkman School next September. I know it will be strange at first, but we're concerned you're missing out on the social aspects of school. How do you feel about that?"

I feel like I just learned your daughter killed the real Vivienne Weir, so feeling strange is relative.

"Cool."

"That's hardly the only news," Mr. Lovecraft says. "Clarissa?"

Mrs. Lovecraft sits next to me and holds my hand. "We'd like to formally adopt you. With your consent, the process will be initiated by our legal team starting tomorrow. Isn't that wonderful?"

Over Mrs. Lovecraft's shoulder, you raise your eyebrows.

. . . . .

By Monday morning, Slade is gone, replaced by Gerry, who is polite and has a beautiful accent and is deadly serious. Before Gerry came to the United States, he was a child soldier in the Lord's Resistance Army under a Ugandan warlord. I don't know the details of Gerry's life beyond the fact that he escaped and was "rehabilitated" and came here, and if anyone wanted to compare our crappy childhoods, I'm betting Gerry wins, hands down.

Unlike Slade, Gerry rejects the idea of sleeping. As far as I can tell, he naps once every day, from four p.m. to six p.m., and requires no more. This allows Gerry to spend a lot of time watching me. I notice when I am being noticed. Gerry looks at me like he understands what being trapped is. This shouldn't make sense, because on the surface, I am the luckiest girl in the world. (Spending money! Car services! Dinners in fancy restaurants!) People dependent on monsters know one another, whether those monsters live in Back Bay or in the bush. When things are quiet, he looks at me this way. The only way to call Gerry out on this is to get him alone, so I wait until Temple is fencing and make up an excuse to go for a walk to the Public Garden.

I start at a pretty good clip, heading down Commonwealth Avenue, crossing at Arlington Street and heading riverward toward Marlborough Street. Gerry walks six paces behind me. I stop and turn.

"Why don't you just walk with me?" I yell.

Gerry stops and shakes his head. "This is where I walk."

"Suit yourself. I don't have a destination, you know. I'm just out here to think."

"Your destination doesn't concern me," Gerry says.

The park on a Wednesday morning has some nannies with strollers and tourists, but it's mostly empty in the way Boston clears out once the college students leave for the summer. I find a spot on a bench near the Ether Monument, a tall fountain-sculpture of a doctor holding a limp, nearly naked man and a cloth coated in ether, which is a pretty miraculous invention when you consider having your appendix out without it, for example.

Anyway. I rarely look up at the naked guy: I prefer the carvings hidden under the arches below, especially the one I'm sitting in front of now, where an angel descends to an injured man.

"Neither shall there be any more pain," I call to Gerry.

His eyes squeeze slightly, considering the inscription's truth. Or doubting it.

I pat the bench next to me. "Come read it yourself."

Gerry plants his feet. "I'll stand here. For your safety."

"You aren't here for my safety. You're here so I don't run away."

Gerry looks on passively. He will not reveal what he knows; he is good at this.

"Suit yourself," I say.

The gurgling lion-faced fountains feed water to the basin. It's a pleasant noise. Gerry is a pleasant—if awkwardly distant—companion, and it feels good to get away from you and my future adoptive parents for a while. It's almost a relief to be with a stranger. To think. I try to make myself feel that Vivi is actually gone. My rational self says, *Jo, you are safe now. No more worrying that the real Vivienne Weir might actually show up.* I should be liking this more than I am. So why won't the darkness lift?

I look toward Gerry and call out, "Is it hard?"

Gerry folds his arms tightly. It's impossible to imagine him folding them any other way.

"Is what hard?"

"Is it hard to feel safe, after everything you've been through? When you were a kid?" I ask.

He looks out the sides of his eyes, as though someone is eavesdropping. Slowly, he walks toward me. Though his gaze fixes on the angel, he is seeing something else.

"When I was abducted from my father, I was still wearing my school shorts. I was a respectful child who prayed and listened to my teacher and my parents. When they took me, they told me they were going to write my name. I thought they would take out a pen. Instead, four teenagers beat me with sticks. They said if I cried out, they would kill me."

"That's awful. That's—"

"That was the beginning. They make you a soldier by three tricks. First, they make you lose hope that you will ever see your parents again."

"Did you try to run back to them? Your parents, I mean."

"If I did I would not be here talking to you."

"Right." I feel my face turn pink. "I'm sorry."

"Second, they make you kill."

I swallow. "Does it get easier, every time you kill?"

"Yes," he says.

I cock my head. I did not expect *yes*, I expected *no*. I expected a lesson. "Because you get used to killing?"

"You do not get used to killing. The first time you kill, you change inside. You think this is a good change, because it brings you respect from the ones who control you. But it is not a good change. You can never go back to not having killed."

I breathe hard. "What's the third trick?"

"They use the rage you have built inside you. Always, a rage so wide that you cannot cross it to get back to yourself."

I picture the insects building inside me until I tilt my head and open my mouth, crossing lakes and mountains, a traveling whorl the length of a football field, then two, whole states and continents. My rage against the Last One could circle the earth twice, a buzzing comet fueled by the million indistinguishable things he did. The humiliations. The frightening near misses in the hotel rooms. The pains he inflicted on Momma.

Behind closed eyes, I remember every violation to my own body.

I picture myself using that rage to kill if I needed to.

"Do you think there's such a thing as a natural-born killer?"

"I know there is not. Killers are made. I have just told you how."

I feel the blood drain from my face, sweet relief. I smile weakly. Gerry registers my gratitude, but does not smile back.

"In answer to your question, Miss Vivienne: I would have to be a fool to feel safe ever again, in my lifetime. I am not a fool. And neither are you."

PART III
JO

The adoption ceremony is held two days later at the Boston Municipal Courthouse, a bustling place. I am dressed up and supposed to be happy, but mainly I'm nervous. The judge is slack-faced and resentful. The Lovecraft name got this done faster or with less paperwork than is typical and the judge knows it, and he is spiteful. I should be happy, but a bitter, contrary thing keeps welling up. Mr. and Mrs. Lovecraft beam. They touch each other constantly, and you roll your eyes, and they talk a lot about how there are families you are born into and families that come together through fate, and that the sadness of the last seven years is 100 percent over, as though something can be 97 percent over, and I want to scream the very definition of over is over. Mrs. Lovecraft says there's something magical about the number seven, and I also want to scream no, that's wrong, it's three, three times makes things so. It's getting hard to hide how opposite I feel, and yet they are so kind, bathing me in love, and it gets even stranger as we walk down the courthouse steps.

In front of the courthouse on busy New Chardon Street parked illegally is Gerry holding a puppy. The puppy licks his face, and he holds it as far away from himself as he can without dropping it, and people crowd around him, which makes him even more uncomfortable than the puppy, and the puppy is that cute.

"Gerry got a puppy?" I say, incredulous.

"No, silly!" says Mrs. Lovecraft, flushing with joy. "It's yours!"

"It's a King Charles spaniel," says Mr. Lovecraft. "A she. Hypoallergenic: we weren't sure if you had allergies."

"She looks like she should be in a calendar," I murmur, eyes fixed on the puppy. "Can I touch her?"

"Can you touch her? You can hold her! She's yours!" Mr. Lovecraft says.

I am cuddling this precious ball of fluff now, and she is shaking, and warm, and something about this sweet creature unlocks my heart, and I am crying into her fur. People around us are making *aww* noises and they might be crying, too, and Mrs. Lovecraft is definitely crying, and

Mr. Lovecraft is swooping us up in his big hug-thing again. I peek out for a moment to see you standing outside our circle, a tightening under your eyes, which are locked on me.

It's been sixteen days since I found the Lovecraft's private investigator's report. Sixteen days, too, since you told me you knew who I was. The four of us live in a strange pretend world where I know the Lovecrafts know I'm not Vivi, but I can't act like it.

Three is my number. Nothing good comes from four.

When I ask you if your parents know I know, you shut me down by saying it's irrelevant: I am theirs now. I do not ask what "theirs" means. If the first part of my time with the Lovecrafts consisted of you giving me experiences, this second half, this After the Knowledge half, is all about the Lovecrafts giving me stuff. In addition to the puppy that still has no name, I have an Apple watch, a credit card of my own, and a hoverboard that only you are capable of riding.

I become their daughter with each accepted gift.

The puppy pees everywhere. Because you complain loudly about the smell, I keep the puppy in my bedroom most of the time. Not including Gerry, you are the only human not brought to your knees by the puppy's adorableness, though this does not surprise me.

"Haven't you named her yet?" asks Zack Turpin every day. I am starting to like Zack more than I did before, possibly because he is the only person who does not seem to want anything from me, and maybe because I'm feeling nostalgic now that I know our time is coming to an end. Zack doesn't even seem to notice that I'm too good at algebra for a kid locked in a shed for seven years.

"I'm calling her Wolf."

"That's cute. She looks like a Wolf," Zack says, and I like him more.

"Can I ask you a legal question?"

"Sure, but I'm not a lawyer yet, so I can't exactly give out legal advice," he says.

"I get that. But what is the advantage of adopting a child when the parents have given you legal custody anyway?"

"Hmm. Well, I guess that's what's so cool about what the Lovecrafts did. There isn't any advantage."

At my feet, Wolf whines in her sleep.

"So why would they do it?"

A strange look passes over Zack's face. "Um, they love you?"

I laugh awkwardly. "Of course, I know they love me. I just wondered: I mean, the Lovecrafts are smart people. Might there be, you know, some financial—maybe a

tax—advantage? Or a legal reason? Something like that."
See, it came outta nowhere, Zack. And in my old world,
the one I spent the longest in, no one does something
without an angle.

"Yeah, there are tax advantages, sure. I don't exactly
think the Lovecrafts are looking to save money on taxes,
though. I guess if there was some reason you got called to
court to testify against them, they'd be safe, because Massachusetts is one of the few states that recognizes parent-
child privilege."

"Say that again?"

"Parent-child privilege. You've probably heard of spou-
sal privilege: that's a big one for TV shows like *Law and
Order*, where someone gets married to avoid testifying
against their spouse. In Massachusetts, a child cannot be
made to testify against a parent."

"So if I knew the Lovecrafts did something against the
law, I couldn't be called to court?"

"Right."

"What if it was something really bad, and they didn't
have any other witnesses?"

"Actually, that's the only time you really hear about that
kind of thing being invoked, in the big cases. You know,
murder, that sort of thing." Zack sits back and runs his hand

through his thinning curls. "Vivi, why are you asking me weird questions?"

I reach down and pull Wolf to my chest and bury my face in her fur. Zack is pure and kind and way too close to the truth, and I'm feeling easily broken these days. "No reason."

"Do you feel like someone is trying to hurt you?"

He says it so tender and kind and tender things must not stay tender, they need to be rubbed until they aren't anymore. When I don't answer him right away, he takes it as not-no, and this is not going in the right direction, not for Zack's own good. "Is it Temple?"

I nearly drop Wolf. "No."

I'm unconvincing, because Zack plows on.

"You know I worked with Temple for a while, right?"

"I didn't. In what subject?"

"English. It wasn't—it wasn't a good fit. I was glad they called me about you. And frankly, a little surprised. Anyway. This probably isn't an appropriate conversation to have. Forget I even brought it up."

"I brought it up."

Zack reaches to scratch Wolf's ears roughly, like she loves. "Yeah. Well. I was talking with my girlfriend about this the other night. I've met people like Temple once or twice in my life. In law school, unsurprisingly." He laughs, as though I ought to get his joke. I frown. "You just need to be careful. There are people in this world who don't feel empathy the same way as other people. They see people as pawns and life as a game to win..I've seen enough of Temple to know that she has some of those qualities. Be careful. That's all I'm saying."

My wrist buzzes: a big no-no during study time. I check my wrist anyway, because I want to hide my reaction to what Zack said.

Tell Zack you're done for the day. I'm out front with an Uber. Getting Starbucks.
And leave the sweater: it looks dorky.

I look down at the lime J.Crew sweater from the day I told the cops I had no memory: the one you told me to wear. I am chilled. For the life of me, I cannot remember if you have seen me today in this sweater. I don't think so, but this is not the kind of thing I would have been unsure of before. What's with all this "unsure"?

I stand. "I have to go."

Zack closes his laptop. "We were done anyway. Promise me something. If you ever feel like you need someone to talk to, someone outside of your family, call me, okay? I'll text it to you."

"No!" I yell. It suddenly occurs to me that they are reading my texts, my e-mails, my search history. Of course they are. Bottom line, Jolene Chastain is a con who cannot be trusted, though they will try their hardest to buy my trust. I push my history book toward him and turn it to page three.

"Write it here," I whisper hoarsely.

. . . . .

"They're making a new hole in the wall."

This is what you tell me later that night over what are not vanilla bean Frappuccinos but rum drinks at Mont Vert, where you know a bartender who thinks we're in college, and the booths are high and private. Gerry waits in the alcove, his face a mask of disapproval.

"What are you talking about?" I say.

You sip your drink neatly and set it back down. "My parents. They say it's to blow insulation in, but you have to wonder." You nod at my drink, called, fittingly, a Crash and Burn. "You're nursing your cocktail. Drink."

I sip. The drink is spicy and I don't like it, but we've done this before—in fact, it's the only place we can do it, and I know you will be relentless until I finish it. The truth is, I like how I feel when I drink with you. It was hard at first to be together, to let you kiss me, but it's easy after a few of these, even though hours later my head feels like a sledge-hammer hit it. Also, it makes me feel like myself: I am the con and I am superior to you and I am still winning. Winning, because I am the one with the house and the clothes and the watch and the adoption papers and the puppy, and the real Vivi is dead, and all I have to do is play along and my life is so much better.

"So do your parents know I know yet?" I ask for the hundredth time.

"Not because I told them. But you should know that Dr. Krebs doesn't believe you're Vivi. Detective Curley's onto you too."

I scowl into my drink. These pieces of news are not things I didn't already suspect.

"Are you just looking for things to worry about? You know what happens if someone tries to out you." With two fingers, you snuff the candle between us. "We're naturals. I told you."

I scowl. I want to be angry with you, but the hot feeling between my legs is there, and the head and the heart are not the same, and alcohol is not my friend. You brush the inside of my arm over and over again with your finger-tips, then kiss my wrist. "You know I'd never let anything happen to you, right?"

I grab your hand hard and you smile. "Let's leave," I say.

"Sorry, I have plans." A man stands over our table. He is dark and hot and dangerous-looking, probably a Boston University student, but when he opens his mouth to say "Let's go, gorgeous," he sounds a lot older.

You rise and walk away, his hand on your waist, never looking back, and I am left, throbbing with want.

. . . . .

They found Zack Turpin shot at an ATM in Brighton. The estimated time of death was ten thirty p.m. I know it is only a coincidence that you stayed out with that random guy until past eleven. I know it is a notoriously dangerous ATM that gets held up all the time and Zack was the kind of guy who would never shrink from the dangerous-looking dude with his hand in his pocket who walks up to the ATM behind him because that would be jumping to conclusions and Zack takes a while to come to conclusions.

I know now that when they finally come, those conclusions are right.

Gerry seems to think Zack's shooting is something we all have to worry about. That it means some greater threat to us. The Lovecrafts are upset in the way rich people get upset when bad things happen to people who serve them. Mr. Lovecraft talks of the dangers of being unaware while in an ATM, as though Zack did something foolish by taking out money. There is much discussion about what to send the fiancée, along the lines of food and flowers and even money, and these are not things Zack would have wanted. Zack would have wanted not to be dead, because he was promising and hopeful in ways I cannot imagine being and he did not do anything wrong.

He did, however, warn me about you.

But Zack is gone and Gerry is here and Gerry insists, in his quiet, respectful way, that we ought to consider Zack's murder as an attack on the family and discuss our current security measures; tighten things up. He calls for a family meeting, which feels pretty ballsy, but Gerry has done ballsier things.

Gerry explains in his oddly formal way why we need to assume lockdown mode.

"Mr. Lovecraft. It has been my experience that enemies

will reach people connected to your family as a message that they are able to get as close to you as they wish. A warning, if you will." Gerry stands rigidly in his fatigues, always in fatigues, long sleeves covering his scarred arms no matter the weather. He and Wolf have scars in common, and my friends are for the most part scarred, and I have started thinking of Gerry as a friend. In Gerry's mind, all of us are under constant threat of kidnapping by the person who kidnapped Vivi, and as a friend, I want to tell Gerry that is hilarious.

Mr. Lovecraft sits in the parlor chair, cupping his knees. "See, Gerry, we appreciate your foresight. Our relationship with Vivi's tutor was pretty tenuous. In fact, he was nearly done working for us. I really don't think—"

Mrs. Lovecraft interrupts. "I can't see how a few more precautions could hurt. Boston is a city. Sometimes I think we forget that. There's always a certain criminal element about, closer than you think."

Your lip curls at me. Mrs. Lovecraft did not mean that at me; she is not intentionally cruel. You, on the other hand.

"Fine. What are you proposing exactly?" Mr. Lovecraft is ready for this to be over.

Gerry blinks slowly; his lids stay down a second too

long. When Gerry first came I did my research, and I know there are things that cannot be unseen, but that the people who abduct child soldiers make them see, and I wonder if this is how he kept from seeing all of it. "The girls. I should stay close to them always. Take them to school. Sleep outside their bedrooms on the third floor."

You roll your eyes. "Overkill," you say, no doubt thinking about Gerry cramping your visits to your little dive bar, and *overkill* seems like an insensitive word to use around Gerry.

"Well, September is months away yet, and we are going on vacation, of course," Mrs. Lovecraft says, eyeing her daughter. "But I can see your point. Particularly if the press make a connection between Vivi and Zack Turpin."

"We appreciate your thinking ahead, Gerry. Being proactive and such. Now," Mr. Lovecraft says, "if you'll excuse me, I brought some work home with me."

"So are we done?" you say.

Poor Gerry. He only wants to do his job well. He does not realize the only threat to Vivi Weir is in this room.

Gerry turns robotically to face you. You actually look startled. "I am thinking of Vivienne. Vivienne is the one who needs my protection the most. Vivienne is the one who escaped."

Mr. and Mrs. Lovecraft lean forward at the same time. "Of course!" they say in unison.

．．．．．

Part of going to the Parkman School in September involves shadowing another student for a day, and that student is not you. In fact, I barely see you during my day with Taylor Washington, who was chosen for her effervescence and love of all things Parkman, and who is shadowing me more than I am shadowing her. Taylor is the model private-school-girl tour guide: on scholarship, so, she is appreciative; ivy league–bound since birth, so, she is focused; and popular, so, she is happy. These things are clear as we move from classroom to classroom, through the hallways, and on to lunch. I, on the other hand, am the model one rumored about: orphaned, so, technically poor; missing since nine, so, uneducated; and maybe-abducted, so, interesting.

The Parkman sweater they gave me to wear for the day itches.

Taylor has the manners to act like I am the most normal girl in the world, even like she has to sell me on Parkman, like I have a choice whether or not to attend. I am vaguely grateful. I don't sense that this is something she was

warned to do: it comes naturally, as will all things requir-
ing good judgment for the rest of her good life. Girls in
private school do not bother with makeup and wear their
hair in sloppy ponytails and buns; this is their privilege, and
to look otherwise is suspect. I am glad I went with as little
effort as possible. Taylor's friends are kind, and they stop
by to greet me and introduce themselves, and I'm slightly
embarrassed because they make a big deal out of me. These
are cool girls—Oona, Lila, and Ming-huá—and Taylor
herself is pretty cool, her eyes a neat shade of amber and
the most perfect skin, and all of these girls are shiny, but
not in a way that is interesting to me. Like you.

On cue, you glide across the dining hall, an airy space
with marked Gluten Free and Vegan selections. Girls who
are not seated with us whisper and stare but the stares are
innocent and I get it. There is golden Temple Lovecraft,
there is poor little Vivienne Weir! How do they deal, when
so much has passed?

If only they knew how much.

You nod at them, all underclassmen and technically beneath you. Taylor stands, as do the rest, and says, "I'm going
to run to the girls' room," and they are gone.

"Looks like you're a hit." You say it so casually. You saw
what a wreck I was this morning, when you scooted out

early but I had to wait to go in with Mrs. Lovecraft and Gerry, God I'm so sick of Gerry, and it felt like you didn't want to walk in together. I want to tell you the only reason I was looking forward to this was to see you in your element, and that has not been the case.

Instead I say, "That might be overstating it. It's nice. Taylor and her friends are nice. The teachers are nice. The classrooms are nice."

"You're showing the strain of all this nice."

I lean in. "It's not what I'm used to."

"You're a con, Vivi." You say this too loud, too carelessly. I check to see if anyone is near enough to hear. "What's that your mother told you? Imagine yourself in another lifetime—a privileged private school student, for example— and become that person."

I cringe. That was one of too many weak moments in the last few weeks, when I told you Momma's theory. I had thought sharing Momma with you would bring her back in a small way. Instead you use it to make me feel like part of a failed carny act.

This time, you lean in. "Not all of us can be intuits."

Taylor appears at my side and you say you'll see me at home, and you thank Taylor for being "so cool about this," as though she's not getting credits or something. Even

Taylor looks embarrassed, and relieved when the next stop is my introduction to "the guidance team," a meeting she is allowed to skip. The team is a man named Brooks Willoughby and a woman named Vonnie Lee, and I am assigned to Vonnie, which is good, since Brooks is fondling his mustache, anticipating getting his hands on my brain. Vonnie closes her office door behind me, an office plastered with posters of small people in front of mountains and canyons and bike trails, suggesting that I Reach and Achieve and Dream. Vonnie has the enthusiasm of a woman just back to the workforce after raising four kids through to college, in her midfifties, grateful for her job, and slightly afraid of her computer. I can use this.

Vonnie shimmies into the seat behind her desk. "Sooo. How is your day going?"

Don't say it, don't say it. "Nice. Everything's . . . nice."

"The Parkman School is a nice place! A welcoming place. A safe place. I am an alumna myself."

"You don't say?"

"Now I won't tell you the year, and do not guess!" she says, waggling her finger. Vonnie, you are shockingly uncool. "I'm sure your parents discussed this with you already, but it may take a while for us to determine the just-right classes for you."

Just-right means not hard: "I understand."

"And of course your 504 plan will reflect the special ac-commodations you require."

"Five-oh . . . special accommodations?"

"An individual plan. For students like you."

"Students like me?"

"We provide every girl an equal opportunity to excel."

"Oh. Huh."

"Let your parents know that I will be sending the draft 504 plan in an e-mail over the next few days. As soon as I figure out how to convert it to a pdf-thingy. No rush, we still have time, but I know they'll want to review it with Dr. Silver."

Okay, so my plan has to do with Harvey Silver's twelve-minute diagnosis. My amnesia. I'm okay with this. This makes sense.

"I will. Um, thanks."

You are waiting against the wall when I leave the guid-ance office. When I ask where Taylor went, you shrug and say you were just trying to be helpful. I ask you what that means.

"I pointed out to Taylor that she had done the majority of what she needed to do today to get to her ultimate goal—volunteer credit, which goes on her application to Princeton—and that doing any more would not help her case. That she was wasting approximately two hours that could be spent doing other work necessary to make her Princeton dream come true: i.e., attend the classics review before finals happening right now. Anyone can be made to do what you need them to do. You have to understand their greatest desire. Once you know it, you have power over them."

This is your gift, knowing which nerve to pluck.

"Or maybe she was just sick of me," I say.

You smile. "Maybe."

Since I don't know where Taylor is, I have nowhere else to go, and my day is over. You realized this, and already called me a car. As I am driven through the Fenway the driver hits a backup in Longwood and makes a turn that leads us all over the city trying to get near Kenmore Square. Boston is layer upon layer of life, parking lots and alleys and networks of underpasses and overpasses, rooftop gardens and filthy sidewalks. The driver grumbles, he does not know this city, has only been here a few days, and I tell him the Citgo sign is our beacon, and finally we turn onto Commonwealth Avenue. I feel the rush of the car more than I should. My world has shrunk, small enough to fit into a snow globe that you shake any time you're in the mood to play.

The spiky parts of you that I've known are there are multiplying, or becoming poisonous in their concentration. I'm not sure which. You prick and withdraw so quickly I'm never sure if it actually happened until I spot the blood. You like to remind me that you hold my perfect life under glass in the palm of your hand, in little ways, like when you sit at the kitchen island and ask in front of the cleaners, or Gerry, if the cops ever found my abductor. Or when you wonder out loud how your diamond earrings went missing but miraculously reappeared in the same spot.

What's most alarming is the way Mr. and Mrs. Lovecraft ignore every one of your strange suggestions. I know that you do not like to be ignored.

While you enjoy threatening me with expulsion, you also enjoy reminding me that I haven't the freedom to leave if I choose. You like to suggest this boy and that boy you know as potential boyfriends under the guise of teasing, but the point is I will never be with Wolf again. You itemize and price the gifts I am given by your parents, cataloging my debt. When we are alone in your bedroom, doing the things we have advanced to doing, you give me side-eyed looks that used to excite me and now make me feel pathetic, as though I cannot help myself from helping myself to you, but you can. You are a table of desserts and I have no restraint. Your faint disgust does not stop me, because I am used to those looks from people on sheets underneath me, though it should.

Not until you pointed it out did I realize how easy it is for some people to kill another person. A quick mental calculation of the danger you are in, of the worth of that life, and your chances for getting away with it. If those things add to the right sum, and you can do it without getting hurt yourself, it's on. Except a person like you doesn't make such calculations. You kill as an attempt to lose control, as an attempt to conjure an irrational state that does not exist inside you, to feel something.

You claim we're alike this way. But we are different, you and me. I am learning.

· · · · ·

Though there are hints of the alarming, truthfully, life is magical these days. On your last day of school, we left Boston for the rest of June and most of July—the girls and Gerry, and Mr. Lovecraft flying back and forth for the weekends—and rented a house on Martha's Vineyard. The Vineyard instead of the usual Nantucket, not because the Lovecrafts were being respectful of Vivi's feelings, but because it would look, as I overheard Mrs. Lovecraft say, "wrong-headed." For the first time in my life, I rode on a boat, which is weird for someone from Florida. The Last One failed on his promises to let me ride on the Everglades boat, same as he failed on his promises to Momma. I don't think of Momma often these days, which is odd since all I have is time. In fact, we are downright lazy, you and I, and the season is passing fast. Though the ocean is still warm, here and there I find a leaf tinged yellow or orange. We do childish things: ride bikes around the island. Reach for the brass ring on the flying carousel at Oak Bluffs. Once, we set our alarms and rose early enough to see the Edgartown lighthouse turn pink at sunrise.

It might have to do with the fact that I am surrounded by the ocean, but you seem less concerned that I am going to leave you and that makes your meannesses fewer and farther between. Mr. and Mrs. Lovecraft are on some kind of *circuit* here on "the island," with parties in Chappy or Squibby every night, and we are left mostly alone. The Lovecrafts had to *reciprocate* all those cocktails, and the one night the rented house was filled with people and the driveway got blocked and you and I escaped to the roof and watched the attendants below scrambling like ants and above I have never seen stars so bright.

I sound more like Vivi these days. How Vivi would sound. I take the Lovecrafts' words in my mouth and try them. See which ones I like. *Reciprocate.*

So much remains of the old you that affection rushes me when I least expect it. The lope of your walk on the sand. The simple swish of your ponytail. The arc of your lower back when you rise and fall on the balls of your feet. The kooky idea that tickles me in its strangeness. These are enough to make me forgive the alarming things you do, the signs that you are getting dangerous.

I should have known it would all come crashing down. The computer at the island house is an expensive design that curves. The owners are a Silicon Valley couple, and they've rigged the house with sensors that play music and trip alarms and turn on the air-conditioning, a network that's supposed to make things easier but causes Mrs. Lovecraft anxiety. The curved monitor is perched on a standing desk in the main room, and in the rare moments when you are not on it, like now, I touch the touchpad just to bring up the screen saver, happy dudes with glowing teeth standing in front of the Acropolis. This time it goes directly to Mrs. Lovecraft's open e-mail, which means you were just reading it. This is how I spot Vonnie Lee's message.

At first I don't want to open it, because you are nearby somewhere, but mostly because the thought of going to the Parkman School in September fills me with dread I can taste. I've barely thought of Parkman, except when we bumped into Lila on the beach and you pretended not to know who she was and things got awkward fast.

But Jo would open it, because information is power, and the one thing I do think of these days is Jo.

The e-mail starts with apologies for its lateness. I can't say I think Mrs. Lovecraft was looking for it, since she rarely read her e-mails. You assumed there was no harm in showing it was read; I, too, doubt your mother would notice. I click on the attachment, which is *For Mr. and Mrs. Lovecraft's review*, and *Edits are welcome!*

Draft 504 Plan in Accordance with Section 504 of the Rehabilitation Act and the Americans with Disabilities Act

Vivienne Weir attends Parkman School and has a diagnosis of "bolting disorder." She is susceptible to fleeing incidents, otherwise known as "wandering," "elopement," or "bolting" (see definition below).

Vivienne is extremely interested in outside attractions, in particular streets and highways and bodies of water. She will wander off to get to these areas, and all measures must be taken to ensure her safety. Due to Vivienne's wandering, her physician strongly urges close and constant one-on-one adult supervision.

Should Vivienne wander, 911 should be called IMMEDIATELY. Parental notification of ANY wandering incident, including incidents where she may have wandered within the building, is required. Incidents should be well documented and include when and how the occurrence took place.

Please know that failure to address known, preventable escape patterns and security breaches puts Vivienne at great risk. We ask for your cooperation in working with us to report all incidents, to make sure the school premises have proper architectural barriers (locks, sensor alarms, and cameras) in place, to ensure all school staff members are aware of her tendency to wander, to ensure fences are gated at all times and exterior doors are always shut, and to ensure that

Vivienne is never left unattended no matter what the circumstance.

To avoid any misunderstanding, Vonnie includes a definition of my "disorder," which I am confident she has lifted from either Dr. Silver or the Internet, or both.

Bolting, also referred to as wandering, elopement, and fleeing, is the tendency for an individual to try to leave the safety of a responsible person's care or a safe area, which can result in potential harm or injury. This might include leaving the classroom without permission.
This behavior is considered common and short-lived in toddlers, but it may persist or reemerge in children and adults. This makes wandering a potentially dangerous behavior.

This is not amnesia, this is something else, something concocted. And I know enough to know that this is something I do not have.

There is even a plan if I should be found bolting:

Call office with name and last location. Office staff will notify all staff, "Code V, Room (last location seen)." When student is located, contact office and all staff will be notified with the announcement "Code canceled."

All staff will look outside their windows and immediate hallway areas. Staff will search second-floor restrooms, work areas, and other nonclassroom areas. Staff will search first-floor restrooms, work areas, gym, cafeteria, and library. Staff will immediately search the outside perimeter of the building.

I am a code: a secret language specific to me if I try to leave school.

Everything in the room—the white tiles, the sea glass on the windowsills, the copper pans hanging from the ceiling—seems to expand and contract every time I breathe.

"Where are you?" you yell from the front hall, carrying in an armful of the blueberry branches that grow in the sandy strip alongside our rented house. "Look what I got to before the birds did!"

Your mouth is stained from the berries and you catch me closing out the open file on the screen. You set the berry branches on the white marble counter and walk to the computer. "Whatcha looking at?"

I swallow, woozy. "I wasn't looking."

One beat, then two. The silence is heavy. Then: "Your life is better now, Vivi. You can't say it's not."

I can't say it. "You're right."

You step behind and put your arms around me to tell me a story, about you and Vivi, the way you can now that I know you know I am Jo. It's one I've heard before, about a boy who bullied all the girls in elementary school with crude suggestions about their "lips"——not the ones on their mouths, and something he'd picked up from porn or an older brother——but especially Vivi, and how you clotheslined him at school, with an actual cord clothesline, and your stories are fun, and I am grateful for this. You even tell me how brave Vivi was, leaning over and spitting in his face, and I know you're making this part up, but it's somehow for my benefit, this mythology about the girl I'm supposed to be.

I cross my hands over my heart and hold your wrists. Just when I am ready to harden my heart to you, you are so sweet. These are the moments when I imagine you and me growing old together, sitting in a café in France or maybe Spain, wearing smart clothes and smoking and being old and cool and free.

That night, slipped under my pillow in the airy loft room I share with you, is a tiny black velvet-covered box with

BARMAKIAN written in gold. I creak it open. Inside is a pair of perfect sparkling diamond earrings, with a note.

The time has come for you to have your own. Kisses, T.

. . . . .

I used to think Wolf liked to come to the Glass Globe because Massachusetts was short on gaudy attractions like Disney World, for example. I never got why anyone would want to see a world map that hasn't been accurate since 1935, but the glass room has one, is one, a "Mapparium" that's really a big, old, hollowed-out, indoor stained-glass planet Earth that you can walk inside. They know Wolf by now and let him in free, and there's always a mass of tourists, so it's easy to get absorbed. Wolf likes to point out that it's the only place where you can see the world without distortion, as it is, with the continents and the oceans all the right size. I never had the heart to point out that, like the audio says, which he's heard a hundred times, even if the sizes are right, the Glass Globe represents a world that doesn't exist anymore, because the political boundaries have changed. There's no Indonesia or Israel, but there is still a Soviet Union and Siam.

I don't have a lot of time. In the two days we've been back in the city, they've been watching me closer than ever.

What Wolf likes best is to watch the workers clean, and that's how I'll find him. A cherry picker sets up on the glass bridge that spans the width, and a worker gets lifted on its arm three stories up to clean each panel with a long broom. Wolf doesn't need to tell me—people are simple—for me to understand that he likes the fact that here, the world can be made clean.

Wolf stands in the dead center of the wide bridge, ignoring irritated tourists who want his prime viewing spot. The lights reflect blue on his bare arms. He's staring at Africa, and his hair fans over the left side of his face, so I cannot read where he is. He coughs into his hand every few seconds, a juicy cough, and people move away. I hold my breath, hanging out by the Indian Ocean, because the Glass Globe is also a whispering gallery where you can hear in Australia things people say in Greenland. Wolf knows my breathing.

I pass right behind him. It is everything I can do not to touch his shoulder as I slip the note into his backpack, but he would startle, the reaction of one used to pickpockets and other kinds of thieves. He will hate this note that puts him on call, that asks him to do, at my bidding, the unthinkable. But when you've done the things Wolf has done, unthinkable is relative.

I have purchased equipment that should make his job easier.

When I finally reach the South Pacific, I make the mistake of looking back. Wolf feels me, snaps his head, but I am off, through the lobby, shoving tourists—always tourists!—through this fairy-tale place, with high arches and lights, but I am less distracted by such spaces than I used to be. Vivi has seen more refined things from the inside than Jo has seen from the outside, and the effect is dulling. Also, I need to escape before Wolf follows me. I cannot explain that note, cannot risk Wolf arguing me out of it. I need him reading that note alone in our tent (if he is still alone in our tent) and remembering his promise to do anything for me.

I am running now across Massachusetts Avenue against traffic and I pass the Symphony T stop because there is no waiting for a train, not with Wolf on my trail, though I got a head start because he had to manhandle those tourists between us on the glass bridge, and for sure the Christian Scientists who built the place aren't letting him into the Mapparium for free anymore. Wolf forces me to run up Mass Avenue, around strollers and students, and it's amazing no cops have stopped us yet, and it helps that Wolf keeps slowing to cough, and I'm faster, one quick turn onto Hemingway and across Boylston, here are the Berklee students moving in sofas and luggage and Wolf won't dare follow me up Newbury, it's too busy, but he does, coughing, and I am panting, and I duck onto Dartmouth and up, up, up the stairs and I don't know if he's still back there but I slam the door anyway and slide down it until I'm sitting on the cold marble.

The fire escape.

I run up the staircase, using the banister to hurl myself up even faster, because my legs are junk, and I rush into my room, fumble with the lock, and slam the cracked window down, locking it shut. There is more danger now, Wolf cannot show up here, and—

"Are you being chased?" you say, laughing, standing in my doorway, your hip jutting out. You're wearing your white fencing knickers and jacket with the strap that goes between your legs. "Maybe I should call Gerry. Gerry!"

I storm out of my room past you because I know you will follow me and I don't need you there when Wolf comes to the window, which he will, and it will be locked. Sweat pours off me. I stick my head in the fridge so I don't have to look at you.

"You didn't tell us where you were going," you say.

"Your parents have been meeting in the office with Gene all morning. I didn't want to interrupt."

"You're full of it. You locked your bedroom door and went down the fire escape. I'm going to tell them to take it down."

"Then how will you sneak out at night to Mont Vert?"

You raise your eyebrows. "Yeah, well, you can't start disappearing now that we're back. It won't be tolerated."

I take out a bottle of orange juice and swig it from the mouth. You wrinkle your nose. When I want space, I do Jo-like things to offend you. We are from different worlds, you and me, but I don't care if you know anymore, and in that way you are losing your power over me.

Puppy-Wolf pads into the kitchen. I scoop her up and bury my face in her warm back.

"You went to see your boyfriend, didn't you?" you say sharply.

I give you my blankest look.

"He doesn't fit into your life now. You know that better than anyone."

"I'm going to lie down," I say, heading for the parlor, which is the last room I spend any time in; that's how badly I want to get away from you. Yet you follow me anyway, and there is the sound of the pocket door to the office sliding open. Lawyer Gene is dragging a hand down his cheek as he emerges. He startles when he sees me. Behind him come Mrs. Lovecraft, Mr. Lovecraft, and Harvey Silver. They mumble hellos and head for their suit jackets on the coatrack by the front door. Mrs. Lovecraft darts into the kitchen for her pocketbook as the men leave.

"Clarissa, I'm leaving my phone, do you have yours?" Mr. Lovecraft yells back.

"Yes!" Mrs. Lovecraft calls. She turns to me. "We need to run an errand. You girls must have lots to do—unpacking, online school shopping?" She looks at me pointedly. "Gerry is here if you need anything."

"All four of you? Together?" you say, as if the weird formality of that needs to be pointed out. This makes you nervous too—something is up—but you care less than I do, and I bet I will find out first.

Mrs. Lovecraft frowns. "I know someone who has a fat math packet that was supposed to be completed by the end of the summer. How far along are you?"

You duck back into the kitchen. I set Wolf on the floor and reach around to hug Mrs. Lovecraft, which I've taken to doing lately because the way she stiffens in my arms reminds me not to be fooled by her. Also, it's easier to slip my hand into the bag on her shoulder and steal her phone.

She can't get away from me fast enough.

I shut down her phone and place it inside the vase on the table in the middle of the foyer. I lift Wolf to my face, light as bones and fur, and breath her sweet doggy smell in, listening for where Gerry is in this godforsaken house. Something about leaving the puppy makes me uncomfortable, but I don't have much time if I want to follow the Lovecrafts, Lawyer Gene, and Harvey Silver to where I think they're going. I use the front door in case the real Wolf is floating around and wait for Lawyer Gene's car to pull away from the curb with the Lovecrafts following behind, a caravan of mysterious intentions. I use my wire cutter to snap the lock on one of the bikes always tied to the meter in front of the Lovecrafts' brownstone and ride as fast as I can toward the police station.

. . . . .

You wouldn't think someone would be able to hang around the window of a police station and hear things. And you'd be right. I stalk the entire station, and though I know where

Detective Curley's office window is, it is barred and painted shut. This was a wrong move, and as soon as you and Gerry discover I'm gone, and call Mr. and Mrs. Lovecraft's phones over and over and don't reach them, I will be screwed without benefit. I am about to mount my stolen bicycle and meet my fate when I see the Lovecrafts, Gene, and Harvey Silver emerge from the station. They decide to debrief at an outdoor café next door, where it is incredibly easy to slump against a wall with my face in my knees, pretending to be homeless.

They sit at a lovely table within hearing distance. Convenient.

"There's nothing Curley can do with a diagnosis. A bolter bolts. That's what they do by definition. We can't conclude that's what happened to Vivienne at nine. But the statement of the social worker is helpful," says Harvey Silver.

"But if the school accepts it, and the social worker accepts it, the police have to accept it, right?" asks Mr. Lovecraft.

"What doesn't help us is the girl's claims when she first came in. Curley can't get those out of his head," says Lawyer Gene.

Harvey Silver rubs his chin. "It would help if the girl

would admit to running away. Are you sure we can't get her to?"

"We've tried," lies Mr. Lovecraft.

"Her attraction to cars and traffic is still apparent. We have to be constantly alert, living on Commonwealth Avenue. You can imagine!" exclaims Mrs. Lovecraft. "We've added bars to our windows. Our private security person is kept busy, I'll tell you that. We let go of our original man because he couldn't be trusted. He didn't understand the endless vigilance required by Vivienne's affliction."

I am sickened.

"Clarissa bears the brunt of it for sure. You just have to hope that Curley can wrap his brain around the fact that Vivienne bolted once before: that foul play wasn't a factor," says Mr. Lovecraft.

A man drops a dollar on the ground in front of me. I stare up at him, my eyes angry slits.

"You know what I'm going to say, Clarissa," says Harvey Silver.

"I know," Mrs. Lovecraft replies. "She's likely to bolt again."

"It would be best if you document her attempts," adds Lawyer Gene.

My heart starts thumping in my chest. Document my attempts?

"You mean in case she succeeds?" asks Mr. Lovecraft.

"Yes, God forbid, in case she succeeds," says Harvey Silver.

Documented attempts. A school aware of my "disorder." A police detective aware of my "disorder."

A new hole in the wall.

The Lovecrafts have gotten what they needed from me: redemption. Now that their daughter has told me everything, Vivienne Weir has become a liability. Where I thought I had the best of them, they had the best of me. A con is another con's easiest mark.

I snatch the dollar from the ground. The Lovecrafts may have made Vivienne Weir disappear, but they won't make Jolene Chastain.

It's time to go back to being nobody.

．　．　．　．　．

The party in celebration of the two-month anniversary of my adoption is to be held at the Christian Science ballroom, home of the Glass Globe. This is your idea, and not a coincidence. I used to think you followed me places—once I was even convinced you had cameras in my room—but I've come to believe you learn things the old-fashioned way. A ticket stub from the Mapparium in my jacket pocket. A phone left on "record" on a shelf ledge during my tutoring sessions. Your techniques are not fancy or sophisticated, but they get the job done, and that is where the con goes wrong, when they try to get too fancy. You're one to watch, Temple Lovecraft.

Anyway.

As best I can tell, this party serves as a big splashy public display of the Lovecrafts' love for me, the love they have crafted. It will make clear to all the pretty people who matter that the only reason I would ever run away (again? Do you think she did that first time?) could be due to a diagnosed illness, a compulsion to bolt

wander

elope

which of course the school knew about, and the police knew about, and Harvey Silver can explain, and what a tragedy. A missing-person case will open, but the Lovecrafts will not worry. They know that the police never look in the walls.

You are in good spirits, because school will start soon, and you do love school, I was wrong that day in the library, about so many things. School is a structured routine and you thrive on routine, where you can prove that you are the best at everything. You are also in high spirits because you love a good party, especially when it is a prelude to a kill.

You shake out your hair in my doorway. "Ready for your 'coming out,' Vivienne Weir?" you ask. You are wearing a black dress that is one-shouldered and sophisticated and you look hot and that makes me cold.

My dress is the color of membranes; a color as raw as I feel. "I'll be there in a second," I reply. When you leave, I smell the white flowers of your perfume, an expensive smell that comes from a black lacquered bottle. I reach into my drawer and pull out the lime-green sweater and ease open my window, my always too-loud window, and lean out, tying the sweater's arms to the railing of the fire escape. The wind makes it hard, weird alley-wind that kicks up and makes no sense, and the sweater gets caught, streaming, less like a flag screaming help than like a skinny girl holding on for dear life.

If Wolf doesn't get my call, he'll see her.

"Vivi, we're going to be late!" Mr. Lovecraft calls, his voice booming.

"Coming, Dad!" I call, shutting the window.

. . . . .

To my earlier point: cons are never focused on the right thing.

In their minds, this night is about what happens next. The Lovecrafts will spend the evening working toward this future-thing, the moment when they get rid of me—later tonight, tomorrow, two months from now—because I became something dangerous rather than something helpful.

They ought to be living in the moment.

If they were living in the moment, they would have seen that my beaded clutch bag is bursting at the seams because of the black tights and a white shirt I have stuffed in there to change into. They would have noticed that I stole Mrs. Lovecraft's credit card and downloaded an Uber app on my phone linked to the credit card. They would have discovered the duffel bag under my bed containing rubber gloves, a half-face respirator, and an ax.

They would have seen the lime-green sweater tied to the railing of the fire escape, rippling in the wind.

But I choose to live in this moment, and for this and other reasons, I wonder who the con really is. I am enjoying the mini tartes flambées and salmon tartare and cucumber cups with vichyssoise, French hors d'oeuvres that I cannot spell, passed in my honor. The room looks magical, with white lights and short candles on tall tables and gauze and glass. And flowers, so many flowers, all white, because there's something virginal about being adopted: a fresh start. The guests' faces are pretty, or else frozen, and sometimes that can be pretty, too. They congratulate me and hold my hands when they do. There is a band playing a mix of old-timey and current music, but I am finding I like the old-timey better, because it suits this fancy place. Gerry is my constant companion, and he would look dashing in his tux if he were not so dour.

You linger at the edges of my vision.

You think of killing as art; on the opposite end of the spectrum is creation. The party is the finishing touch. At least that's how it seemed earlier. But now something is bothering you; even across the room, I have witnessed a swing from manic socializing to dark lurking. I suspect it is me enjoying myself. I suspect you see me relaxed. I no longer act trapped, because I know I am leaving soon.

The good con feeds on other people's mistakes.

I have no room for mistakes. I extract myself from a dull conversation with a horse-faced couple and cross the room to you drinking a third glass of champagne after

Mr. Lovecraft took the first and then the second from your hand. Around us, people laugh and talk.

"This is the worst night of my life," I say.

"You seem to be enjoying yourself," you say accusingly.

"It's hard—" I start.

"Being Vivi?" you ask. "Because of Mrs. Weir's relatives being here? Yes, I imagine it is. Of course, you're lucky they live abroad and never saw Vivi much. There's that."

I nod. I will let you fill in the rest, what you think my discomforts are. What you want them to be.

"I imagine it's hard for you to fake stuff like this. Basic etiquette stuff, like how many hors d'oeuvres to take, returning glasses to trays. How to politely leave a conversation."

You needed so little to figure me out. But I needed so much from you.

"You don't even know who's important in this room. Like over there: that's Dick and Anne Marie Connolly." She nods at a handsome couple surrounded by other couples across the room. "The Boston Symphony Orchestra couldn't operate without them. That guy? John Fish, Fish Construction? Dad's closest competitor. Keep your enemies close, right?"

I look for Gerry, recessive Gerry, who is standing on a

high level behind a railing now, watching us. That's the kind of distance I've been waiting for all night, and now I'm caught in a conversation with you. I check my watch, which I insisted on wearing with my dress, though Mrs. Lovecraft gave me the stink-eye, calling it "indelicate."

"I usually do," I say.

You like that, when I admit to my con tricks, and you soften, wrapping your arm around mine. "I'm sorry, Vivi. I know things have been strange between us lately. It will get better."

Until it doesn't. Until you decide that killing me is a good way to make your parents sweat it out like they have for the last seven years, or until you convince them that my knowledge, the knowledge you gave me, makes me too dangerous. Or maybe it's just until you have to answer to your bloodlust. Your parents know that one of these things may happen, will happen, and they've set it up once again for you to get off, free. It doesn't matter. I am not waiting around for one of these motives to take hold; I will not find myself rattling bells inside your wall.

You lean into my ear and say, with predictable kinkiness, "After all, we're sisters now."

Mr. Lovecraft approaches. He wears a pink pocket square that matches my dress, and Mrs. Lovecraft, in tasteful silver-gray, waits a few feet behind, talking with a woman responsible for making sure things run smoothly. "It's time, girls."

He holds out both his arms, and you take one and I take the other and we float to the stage, and this shouldn't feel as nice as it does. My face is hot, and I wish you had been especially cruel this time, because I need fresh pain to remind me why I am running. Momma said if wishes were horses, beggars would ride, and she was right, wishing is for the common and the hopeless. I need to stop wishing and make things happen.

The band finishes its last song and the warped sound of a standing mic being repositioned blares over the room. This is it. I will be introduced, kind things will be said, and it will all be a streaky blur. Then I get to step down and sit with my parents at our table and for exactly eight minutes, the director of Adoption America will talk, and this is when I disappear. Mr. Lovecraft speaks first, his women by his side (and I am one of these), and he speaks touchingly of how I came into their lives, and left, but now I am back, and nothing else matters. If I really was Vivi, I bet Vivi wouldn't agree, because being locked in a shed for seven years matters when it comes to everything.

He wraps up his speech by staring at the podium for a count of ten.

"A man doesn't always get a chance in life to set things right when they go wrong. But on behalf of myself, and Clarissa and Temple, I venture to say that this city has been handed a miracle." He pauses, this time, for a count of five. "And her name is Vivienne Weir."

They are crying. The audience is crying. John Fish is applauding and ugly-crying. Dick Connolly is raising his glass to me. My hands are blocks of ice. Do they expect me to say something?

And as Mr. and Mrs Lovecraft hug me and sob, you step to the microphone. It takes everyone a minute to regain themselves, but they do, and you wait for them, poised and perfect as that first day I saw you in your carrel with your poems. You hold a folded piece of paper.

The microphone whines. You readjust it to your height with one hand, and it is awkward, and I want to help you, damn me.

"Hi everybody. For those who don't know me, I'm Temple Lovecraft," you say, in a voice younger and smaller than your own. Humble is the way to go tonight, you have decided, and it hits the right note, because already people are oohing and aahing because Temple is going to speak and she looks darling and she's gotten so big and what character she must have, to be composed during such a strange time.

"I wanted to read a poem in honor of Vivi coming home. It's by Emily Dickinson, and it's a favorite of ours." You pause and smile at me shyly. "It goes like this: 'A death blow is a life blow to some, who till they died did not alive become. Who had they lived, had died but when they died, Vitality begun.'"

You pause dramatically.

"To me, this speaks to a second chance for Vivi, and for all of us. We're so blessed." You turn to me with bright, glassy tears. "I'm so glad to have you home, Vivi." You hug me, and we rock, and you are crying and laughing, for a solid minute, it seems, and the guests are now heaving with collective sobs, and I am thinking this is it, you are right, this is my home. This room loves me. This room loves us. I don't know for sure that you're going to hurt me; it's natural that you should be a little jealous, I mean, they're having a coronation for me. You have confessed things that scared me, but I have known worse, have loved worse. Wolf told me he fantasizes every single time about killing the men he is with. I imagined training pigs to devour the Last One's flesh.

Still.

While the others sit, I excuse myself and head into the bathroom to pull myself together. The door swings and a maid holding towels in the corner shuffles out. I throw my bag on her empty chair and weep. I have set Wolf on a path and I have no way of letting him know we have to stop, that this was all a mistake, this is a world I can live in, even if it means keeping constant watch on you.

I look into the mirror and pull my hair away from my face at the temples. "Who are you?" I hiss.

A man slips into view behind me. I nearly scream.

Gerry tries to hand me the clutch I abandoned on the chair. "It's time to go," he says, in that elegant voice.

I spin to face him. "What do you mean?"

He nods at my bag. "I will lie, say you feel sick and are getting some air, but that you are watched by me and there is no worry. When I return, I will tell them you have escaped. Go."

I rub a streak of mascara across my cheek with the heel of my hand. "I'm not going. This is where I belong. This is my life now."

"A life never knowing when you are going to die is not a life worth living," he says.

Tears well, and tears are like wishes: useless. "None of us know when we're going to die," I say.

"Let me put it differently. People will pretend to be your

comrades. They will make you do things that braid them to you. But because you did these things does not mean you are these things."

Gerry is right and you are wrong. I am not a natural-born killer. If I was, I would have killed the Last One back in that hotel room the night he killed Momma.

"I have seen the eyes of girls who want to die. For them, it would be better. These girls are not you." Gerry looks at the door. "This is your last chance. Go." He looks at his watch. "You have six minutes."

I turn to the mirror. I don't want to die.

Gerry thrusts the clutch at me. I grab the clutch from his hand, fumble for the phone, and call the car. He nods and leaves as quietly as he came, and I pull my dress over my head, stashing it in the trash can. The black pants and white shirt work perfectly—instantly, I am catering staff—and I slip from the ballroom and into the night while applause roars down behind.

· · · · ·

By the time I reach the town house in my Uber I am in a full-on panic. The phone started ringing wildly, and I pitched it out the window before we made the turn off Huntington. My best calculation has the Lovecrafts—or the cops they call—arriving at the town house between four and eight minutes behind me. If Wolf has not finished his job, we are done.

I fumble with my key. With the lights off, the town house is eerie. The puppy runs to me and pounces at my feet. I grab her and stuff her in my shirt. Wolf appears in the door frame wearing his respirator, like something out of an apocalypse movie. His clothes are covered in plaster and he holds the duffel in one gloved hand. It sags with the weight of its contents. Beyond, I see the gash Wolf has chopped in the wall, and the ax on the floor, its blade powdered with plaster.

I stare at the duffel too long. Longer than we have.

"She's inside?" I say.

Wolf nods, wild-eyed.

I gather my courage and shake off the fear. "Then we can go," I say.

Wolf peels off his mask and heads for the front door.

"No!" I yell, and run up the stairs, and he follows me to my bedroom and out the window and onto the fire escape. "They're right behind," I huff, steadying the puppy squirming at my neck.

We stay in the alleys and the shadows and unlit store-fronts, making our way across the city to the waterfront.

It is far and hard and long, and we duck every time we hear sirens, and we hear sirens a lot. Wolf suffers under the weight of the duffel, under the weight of her bones, and I have to help, but I can't help while holding the dog, and so I let her go. She follows us for a while until she can no longer keep up. I don't look back at her, because if I do, I will stop, and there is no stopping. When I take the bag from Wolf, I am surprised at how much bones and hair and scraps of material weigh. When I slow, I imagine Vivi wanting us to go faster. I feel the pull of Vivi, the way she refused the fate the Lovecrafts had given her, biding her time until I came along to free her. "Don't stop," I hear her saying in her little-girl voice, and I run faster, am lighter, more agile, dodging the streetlamps and headlights that make us look like the fugitives we are. The first whiff of the ocean hits us as we get to the end of deserted State Street and cross the highway to Atlantic Avenue, exposed and broad, with no alleys and night workers in hard hats. It is the only way to Seaport Boulevard, but we get there, then cross to Northern Avenue with its accusing lampposts staring down upon us from both sides.

Wolf staggers, breathing hard. Maybe he has begun smoking again or is having a reaction to the plaster dust. Either way, he needs to move if we're going to make it to the ship in time. We have no clothes, but we have stolen mad money and a bag full of bones that are enough evidence to keep the Lovecrafts from chasing me for the rest of my life. A turn onto Tide Street, then Drydock, and Wolf is nailed by a coughing spasm, and I yell for him to move ahead of me so I can push him along. When his hand dangles at his side, I see a flash of bright blood he coughed into his palm.

We reach the Black Falcon terminal just as the ship calls final check-in. We move through empty lines marked by velvet ropes. Fat couples belly up to the deck rails, too full of anticipation to show us much attention. I shove my tickets bought with money stolen from the Lovecrafts, my inheritance, into a bored man's hand, along with our fake IDs. We are made to fill out a form promising we haven't been sick lately. I kick Wolf to straighten up, and he shoves his bloody hand in his pocket. We look like a young couple crazed by the thought of missing our cruise, I tell myself. We ran into traffic on 93, I tell the man with a giggle. We are so psyched for this vacation. My husband needs it, he came straight from a carpentry job, didn't even have time to change clothes. We would have been *sooo* bummed to miss our only vacation, in, like, forever!

Wolf puts his free hand on my hand holding the duffel. I was swinging it, hard, without realizing. I clear my throat.

The man points to a tiny camera where our pictures are taken and we are given "cruise cards" in the names of Patrice and Charlie Silver. Pretty names that I stare at a second too long. The cruise cards will get us into our room, and pay for our meals, and give us handy-dandy schedules of each day's events, including Zumba and mah-jongg. But the Silvers will not leave their room. The Silvers (with their guest beside them) are going to sleep for a long time.

We scramble up the gangway and follow directions to our room, a crappy, tiny thing on the lowest deck. Wolf is pale and I want only to get him into a bed with a shower going to make steam. I know the TB cough from Tent City, and I know Wolf's lungs, already weak from infections, will not stand up to it. When we turn the corner, I stop and feel his flaming forehead. I nearly knock him over. He falls to the bed and is asleep before I turn on the shower.

The duffel sits where I left it on the carpeted floor next to the door. Wolf breathes, wet and sticky.

"Okay then," I whisper. "It's just you and me. I want you to see something."

I hoist the duffel onto my shoulder, wincing at the rattle of shifting bones inside, and close the cabin door softly behind me.

. . . . .

You're wondering if I threw Vivi's bones overboard.

It took me five sets of stairs and landings before I found a length of rail unoccupied by cruise-goers taking selfies and making clichéd remarks about the tiny lights of Boston Harbor and the black nighttime sea.

I opened the zipper partway and held up the bag. It was the first of many times that I have spoken to her since. "Can you see, Vivi? That's the ocean. The real ocean, not the slice of it that you see from the beach. It's a dark place that you can get lost in, which is exactly what we need right about now. I don't know if you got to see it in your lifetime, but I'm pretty sure you did.

"A friend once reminded me that I didn't want to die. And I know you didn't either. We have that in common.

"We're going to be friends now, you and me. And I'm going to teach you something that my momma taught me. The only thing we have to fear in this whole wide world is not remembering. I didn't remember who I was for a while, and it got me in trouble. I am Jolene Chastain, and you are Vivienne Weir.

"I am Jolene Chastain. I am Jolene Chastain. I am Jolene.

"And we're going on a trip, Vivi. Wolf won't last, but you and I will. We will be together forever."

After that I gave her a good long look at the ocean before I zipped her back up, which felt cruel.

. . . . .

You never came to get me. According to the police report, when you and your parents and the police saw the hole in the wall, you were the one smart enough to yell, "Someone stole the safe!" Quick thinking, you. So many pieces had been put into place, it was easy to pin my disappearance on my bolting disorder, the culmination of a day of excessive stimulation. The damage to the parlor wall was an everyday Back Bay B and E. I have to think Detective Curley is spending his retirement working on both cases in his spare time, combing over the facts at his dining room table under an old cuckoo clock. The clock will chime, and he will still have no answers, day in, day out. He will die frustrated.

Montreal is the New York City of Canada. It's where

people go to lose themselves and become new people. The problem with cities like Montreal and New York is that you're always running into new transplants with ambitions, and as I've learned, those are dangerous. Better to accept who you are in this life and get on with it. That's what I figure Gerry did; covered up his betrayal, and stayed working for the Lovecrafts. Gerry knows true evil, whether it's in the bush or Back Bay, and he can make a home inside it and survive.

When you accept who you are, you can tap the brakes when you feel yourself veering toward your worst tendencies. For example, every time I want to pretend that I know French, I bite my tongue. I am proud of my new self-control. I have a job waitressing at a place called Frites Alors where they serve grilled cheeses with apples and honey and french fries with mayonnaise and when I go home, Vivi is there, waiting. She lives in a Lucite box now—the duffel bag encased in a Lucite box, that is—because I couldn't imagine what would happen if I couldn't get all her parts out during the transfer. She is my insurance, my most valuable thing, and you keep valuable things protected. We talk every night, and she is a good listener.

I kept the Tiffany charm bracelet. I kept it to remind me I am someone's daughter. That person was Patrice Chastain. I had a mother once, and she loved me.

I try not to keep up with you. But in weak moments, I do. The Google Alert I have on your name pings a lot. You graduated, then took a gap year, but that doesn't mean you're not doing stuff. You've started a charity in my—Vivi's—name, dedicated to "raising awareness of bolting/eloping behaviors." It's a nice touch. I read Fish Construction made a grant of a million dollars to endow it. I still don't know if you ever would have killed me, and sometimes it's okay not to know things.

I have a new dream. You chase me down the Black Falcon pier and the gangway pulls up just as you reach it. I am the only passenger. You stand on the dock, your father's coat wrapped around your black dress twice, hair whipping around your face. You cup your hands around your mouth and yell, "Vivi!" and your voice is carried off by the wind. Leaning over the churning sea, you mouth something else, three words, but I can't make them out. If you can't hear something, three times doesn't make it so. I turn to walk below deck.

Again, you call, "Vivi!"

And I keep on walking, because I remember that my name is Jo.

ACKNOWLEDGMENTS

In *In Her Skin*, Jolene Chastain believes her destiny in life is to have "that family." I have that family at FSG/Macmillan, and they must be thanked.

Janine O'Malley planted the seed for Jolene's story. All authors should be so lucky to have an editor with a perfect sense of the stories they want—and need—to tell. I'm grateful for the gifts a stellar editor gives, but especially for the space Janine gave me, at the end, that I needed in order to get *In Her Skin* right.

My publicist, Morgan Dubin, and the team at Fierce Reads continue to shout about my work (in the most lovely ways) when this introvert shies from doing so. My gratitude cannot be overstated.

Speaking of family, writing partners become sisters, and I have two. Thanks to Larisa Dodge, for reminding me to make time to shuffle around in my father's old sweater. It was the best advice a grieving daughter could get. And to Candace Gatti, who believed mightily in *Beautiful Broken Girls*, and hand-sold it, everywhere. Her generosity on my behalf is breathtaking.

Thanks, too, to the collective wisdom of Binders Full of Young Adult Writers, who shared how they write through grief with candor and wisdom.

My dear friend Mary Larkin Quinn lent her considerable expertise on bolting, and another dearest, Kelley Byron St. Coeur, introduced me to the remarkable students of Boston Latin Academy, a group of sophisticated thinkers who sparkle in real ways. The Parkman School is not Latin Academy, but I was inspired by the brilliance of its students.

My agent, Sara Crowe, has a gift for identifying superfluous characters and story lines. *In Her Skin* is infinitely better for her earliest guidance. Thanks, too, to the team at Pippin, the most welcoming and supportive literary agency a writer could want.

Cristy Walsh trained her artistic eye on the renovation of my home so that I could write, and only write.

Jackson, Charlie, and Lila soothed my soul while I finished this novel. Lila, this is your book. There's no better you than the you that you are, but you know that. Always know.

In Her Skin is, in fact, a novel about the danger of forgetting who you are. I have a husband who, in gently reminding me to get back to work, reminds who I am foremost: a writer. Gary, I love you.

Writers stand on other writers' shoulders. Jolene is an homage to one of my favorite fictional characters, Shirley Jackson's Merricat Blackwood. Merricat would say three times makes it so.

I thank you, I thank you, I thank you.

Don't miss these other mysteries by

Kim Savage

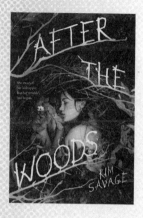

★ "A riveting exploration of what it's like when the enemy is much closer than you suspect."
—*KIRKUS REVIEWS*, STARRED REVIEW

"An intense, dark, staggering debut."
—**PASTEMAGAZINE.COM**

★ "The mystery unfolds with aching precision . . . Mesmerizing."
—*KIRKUS REVIEWS*, STARRED REVIEW

"A haunting tale that reads like a young adult version of Jeffrey Eugenides's *The Virgin Suicides*. Give to fans of Jay Asher's *Thirteen Reasons Why*."
—**SCHOOL LIBRARY JOURNAL**

"A mystical secret nobody had anticipated." —*TEEN VOGUE*

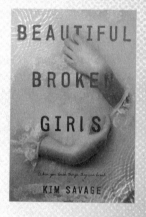

SQUARE
FISH

fiercereads.com